The Apostle

A Southern Outer Banks Novel

BOBBY BRYAN GOODWIN

Core Sound Media LLC

First Edition

eBook ISBN: 978-1-971321-03-5
Paperback ISBN: 978-1-971321-04-2
Hardcover ISBN: 978-1-971321-05-9

Published by Core Sound Media, LLC
www.coresoundmedia.com

For my grandfather,
The Reverend Lemuel Gibbons Roberson, Jr.
who gave me a book for Christmas 1982 and wrote inside,
"I have a feeling you will write your own one day."
His words stay with me.

Contents

Chapter One

The Fisherman

He becomes aware of the water before he becomes aware of himself.

The boat is moving. He feels it before he understands it: the slow, steady glide beneath his feet, the faint hum of the trolling motor carrying them forward. He is standing on the bow of his Pathfinder, barefoot on the casting deck, the rod already in his hands. Cool and damp. He doesn't remember stepping onto it.

The marsh slides past on his right. Marsh grass, thick and tall, glowing a pale lime green in the early light. He knows this place: the shallow bay where the water thins over sandy mud, grass and shell, where redfish tail in the shallows and herons stand like gray sentinels at the water's edge. He has worked this shoreline more times than he can count. Since his college days. Since before he understood that some places become part of you.

But something is different this morning.

The sky.

He looks up, and his breath catches.

The sun has not yet broken the horizon, but the light is already filling the sky in ways he has never seen. Colors that don't belong to dawn: deep golds bleeding into violet, ribbons of pale rose and amber stretching across the water. The light seems to come from everywhere and nowhere, pooling in the mist that hangs low over the marsh, turning the marsh grass luminous.

It is the most beautiful morning he has ever seen.

And he knows, somewhere beneath thought, that this is not real. That mornings do not look like this. That he is dreaming.

But knowing doesn't diminish it. If anything, it makes the colors sharper, the silence deeper. He is inside something sacred, and he doesn't want to wake.

The water is still. Unnaturally still. Glass-smooth even though he can feel a faint breeze on his face, a breeze that should be rippling the surface but isn't. The boat glides forward and leaves no wake. The marsh reflects in the water like a mirror, unbroken, and he cannot tell where the water ends and the sky begins.

No gulls. That's what's missing. This time of morning, they should be making their first flights, white shapes wheeling against the pink sky, their cries carrying across the sound. But there is nothing. No splash of mullet. No rustle in the grass. Only the faint hum of the motor and the slow passage of the boat through water that feels more like glass than liquid.

The silence presses against him. Expectant. As if the whole world is holding its breath.

He casts toward the marsh edge. The lure arcs out over the shallows and lands softly, just where the water meets the grass. He works it back slowly, twitching, pausing, reeling, the way he has done ten thousand times.

Nothing.

He casts again. Same spot. Same rhythm. The lure moves through water so clear he can see the sandy bottom, the thin shadows of his line. No fish. No movement. Nothing.

A flicker of frustration rises in his chest. Not because he expects to catch anything, this is a dream after all, but because the stillness feels like it's waiting for something, and he doesn't know what.

He reels in. Casts again. The marsh glides past, beautiful and silent and strange.

Nothing.

"Try the other side."

The voice comes from behind him. Quiet. Unhurried. As if the man has been there all along. And there's something in the voice, a familiarity he can't place. Not the words themselves, but the tone. The cadence. As if he's heard this voice before, in some other context, some other life. It unsettles him in a way he can't name.

He turns.

The man is sitting on the bench seat behind the center console. Elbows on his knees, hands loosely clasped. Ordinary clothes: worn, comfortable, the kind a man wears when he's not trying to impress anyone. His face is turned toward the horizon, toward that impossible sky, and there is a stillness about him that matches the water.

Lem doesn't startle. He feels no fear. Only a strange, quiet recognition, as if this were how the morning was meant to be.

"Try the other side," the man says again.

Lem lets out a breath, half laugh, half sigh. "That's not how it works."

The man tilts his head slightly, waiting.

"The fish are in the shallows this time of morning. Along the edge. That's where they feed." He gestures toward the marsh with the tip of his rod. "You don't cast into deeper water. There's nothing out there."

The man's expression doesn't change. A small smile. Patient. Knowing.

"Try the other side."

"I've fished this water my whole life." Lem hears the edge in his own voice now, defensive in a way he doesn't fully understand. "If there was something there, I'd know."

A pause. The boat drifts forward. The marsh slides past like a slow green dream.

The man's eyes soften.

"You know many things," he says gently. "But not everything."

The words land somewhere deep, deeper than they should. Lem feels something tighten in his chest, a small knot of resistance, of pride, of fear.

He looks back at the water. The deeper water, off to the left. Dark and still. Empty.

"It won't matter," he says.

"Try."

He stands there a moment longer, the rod in his hands, the weight of the man's gaze on his back. The sky blazes above him in colors that have no name. The boat hums forward through the silence.

He exhales slowly.

"Fine," he mutters. "But don't say I didn't tell you."

He turns to the left side of the boat. Faces the deeper water, away from the marsh, away from everything he knows. The water out there is darker, the bottom invisible. It feels wrong. Every instinct he has says the fish aren't there.

He casts anyway.

The lure arcs out over the dark water and lands with a soft splash.

The line goes taut instantly.

Not violently. Not the savage strike of a big fish. Just a steady, living pull that travels up the rod, through his hands, into his chest. He feels it in his whole body: the aliveness of it, the weight and motion of something real on the other end of the line.

He reels in slowly, hand over hand, the way his father taught him when he was small. The fish doesn't fight. It comes toward the boat as if it wants to be caught, as if this was always the plan.

It breaks the surface, and he gasps.

The fish is silver, trembling, catching the strange light of the sky. But something is wrong. The scales are too bright, reflecting colors that aren't in the water, aren't in the sky, aren't anywhere. It's as if the fish is catching light from somewhere else entirely. Some other sun, some other dawn.

For a moment he forgets everything else. The wrongness of the morning, the man behind him, the fact that this is a dream. There is only the fish, impossibly bright in the strange dawn.

He kneels at the rail.

The casting deck is hard under his knees as he bends over the gunwale, the fish cupped in both hands. Water drips through his fingers. He can feel its heartbeat, or maybe that's his own. The rapid pulse of something small and frightened and alive.

The fish breathes against his palms. Gills working. Body flexing. Insisting on life. And still that brightness, not glowing, not supernatural, but *too much*. As if all the beauty of every fish he's ever caught has been concentrated into this one small body.

"Thank you, God," he murmurs.

The words come without thought, the way they always have. Every fish, since he was a boy. His father's voice first, then his own. The habit of gratitude so old it lives in his hands.

He lowers his arms into the water, letting the cool of it rise past his wrists, and opens his fingers.

The fish holds still for a moment, stunned or resting, he can never tell. Then it flicks once, twice, and vanishes into the dark.

He stays there, kneeling, watching the last ripple fade. The water goes still again. The sky burns above him.

"People spend their entire lives trying to reach God's kingdom."

The voice is beside him now.

Lem doesn't turn. Doesn't startle. In the way of dreams, it feels right that the man is there, kneeling next to him at the rail, both of them looking out at the water, shoulders almost touching.

"They chase it. Pray for it. Wait for it." The man's voice is quiet, unhurried. "They look to the sky, or to the next life, or to someone else to bring it to them."

The boat drifts forward through the silence. The marsh glows green and gold. The colors in the sky deepen, beautiful beyond bearing.

"But the kingdom is not far away. It is not later. It is not somewhere else."

A pause. When the man speaks again, his voice is low. Tender.

"It is here."

The words settle over the water like morning mist.

Lem swallows. His throat is tight.

"The kingdom of the Father is spread out upon the earth," the man says, "and people do not see it."

Something shifts inside him. Not understanding, not yet. But recognition.

He turns his head.

The man is looking at him. Close. So close he can see the light reflected in his eyes, the fine lines at the corners, the steadiness of his gaze.

A face he recognizes.

His breath catches.

His hand reaches out.

And he wakes in the dark, his arm outstretched, his fingers trembling.

* * *

For a moment he doesn't know where he is.

The ceiling is faintly visible, a dim gray rectangle in the thin spill of streetlight through the blinds. His heart is pounding. His breath comes in shallow gasps. His arm is still extended, reaching for something that isn't there.

He lowers it slowly. His hand falls to the sheet.

His face is wet.

He blinks. Touches his cheek with his fingertips. Tears. His pillow damp beneath his head.

He wasn't sad. He wasn't grieving. But something in him, something deeper than thought, older than language, had wept.

The dream hasn't faded. That's what frightens him. Dreams dissolve. He knows this, has known it all his life. You wake and reach for them and they slip away like water through your fingers. But this one sits inside him whole and heavy, every detail intact. The colors of the sky. The glowing marsh. The man's voice, low and certain. The face.

The face.

He closes his eyes and tries to see it again, but it's already blurring at the edges, the features slipping away even as the feeling remains. He knew that face. He's sure of it. But from where? From when?

He raises his hands to rub his eyes, and stops.

His hands smell like fish.

Faint but unmistakable. The salt-and-silver smell of a fresh catch, the smell that lives in the grain of his skin after a morning on the water. He brings his palms closer to his face, breathes in. It's there. Real. The smell of the fish he held in the dream.

That's not possible.

He lies still, his hands hovering near his face, his heart beating too fast. Dreams don't leave smells behind. Dreams don't follow you into the waking world.

But the smell is there. And he cannot explain it away.

The warmth beside him shifts.

Beth turns toward him, one hand tucked under her cheek the way she's slept for thirty years. Her eyes are closed. Her breathing slow.

"Hey," he whispers. His voice is rough. "You awake?"

She stirs. A small sound, barely conscious. "Mm?"

"I had a dream."

She doesn't open her eyes. "Mm-hmm."

"It was different. More real than..." He stops. The words feel inadequate. Foolish. "There was a man. On the boat with me. We were fishing, and he told me to cast on the other side, and I caught something, and then he..."

"You've been stressed," she murmurs. Her voice is thick with sleep. "Dreams get weird when you're stressed."

"It wasn't like that."

She's silent. Maybe already asleep again.

"It felt like it was actually happening," he says. "Like he was really there. Like he was trying to tell me something."

She reaches over without opening her eyes, her hand finding his arm, patting it gently. "It was just a dream," she says. "Go back to sleep."

He nods in the dark. Because it's easier than explaining. Because he doesn't have the words yet. Because how do you tell someone that you just woke up from the most beautiful morning of your life, and it didn't happen, and you're crying, and you don't know why?

She turns away, pulling the blanket up over her shoulder.

He lies still, staring at the ceiling.

After a moment, her voice comes again. Softer. Already fading.

"Your pillow's wet."

He doesn't answer.

Her breathing slows. Deepens. She's gone.

He reaches up and touches his face again. His cheeks. The dampness cooling in the dark.

Then he brings his hands back down and smells them again. Still there. Fainter now, but still there. Fish. Salt. The sea.

He lies awake for a long time after that.

The dream plays behind his eyes: the water, the light, the man's voice beside him at the rail. *The kingdom of the Father is spread out upon the earth, and people do not see it.* He doesn't know what it means. Doesn't know who the man was, or why his face felt so familiar, or why his whole body aches like homesickness for a place he's never been.

It was real. More real than this room, this bed, this ceiling. More real than anything he's felt in years.

And he knows, with a certainty that settles into him like stone, that it wasn't just a dream.

The tears dry on his face.

He doesn't sleep again that night.

* * *

Chapter Two

The Morning After

He doesn't remember coming downstairs.

One moment he's lying in bed, staring at the ceiling, the gray light of early morning pressing against the blinds. The next he's standing in the kitchen, his hand on the coffee pot, the warmth of it seeping into his palm.

He slept, finally. An hour, maybe two. But the dream didn't return. He lay awake waiting for it, wanting it, dreading it, and it never came. Just the dark, and the sound of Beth breathing beside him, and the slow crawl of hours until the light began to change.

Now the coffee is made. He doesn't remember making it.

The kitchen is quiet. The house is quiet. Through the window over the sink, the bay lies flat and silver in the early light. The dock stretches out from the shore, the Pathfinder tied at the end, rocking gently. The marsh beyond, green and gold, catching the first touch of sun.

He pours a cup. Holds it without drinking. Watches the steam rise and curl and disappear.

The dream is still there. Not the images anymore. Those have blurred at the edges, the colors fading like an old photograph. But the weight of it. The presence. The man's voice, low and certain: *The kingdom of the Father is spread out upon the earth, and people do not see it.*

He looks out at the water. The same water. The same marsh. But ordinary now. Just the view from his kitchen, the view he's seen every morning for fifteen years.

Where did it go?

Footsteps on the stairs. He turns.

Beth comes into the kitchen already dressed: slacks, a light blouse, her hair pulled back. She moves with purpose, the way she always does when she has somewhere to be. He watches her cross to the cabinet, pull down a mug, pour her coffee. She turns and leans against the counter, studying him over the rim.

"You look tired," she says.

"Didn't sleep well."

"The dream?"

He nods. Takes a sip of coffee to fill the silence.

She watches him a moment longer. "What was it about? You never really said."

He opens his mouth. Closes it. How do you describe something that felt more real than the room you're standing in? How do you explain colors that don't exist, water that doesn't ripple, a face you recognized but can't name?

"Just a strange dream," he says finally. "A man on the boat with me. It felt... real."

She tilts her head slightly, waiting for more.

But there is no more. Not that he knows how to say.

"You've been under a lot of pressure," she says. "The deadline. The outline. You're not sleeping well, you're not eating well. It makes sense your brain would be working overtime."

He nods. She's right. She's always right about things like this.

"Maybe lay off the coffee after noon," she adds, a small smile softening the suggestion. "And try to get some pages down today. Even rough ones. Just to get moving."

"I know."

She sets her mug in the sink and crosses to him, reaching up to touch his face. Her palm is warm against his cheek. "You'll figure it out. You always do."

He wants to believe her. He tries to.

She kisses him lightly and turns to gather her things: keys, purse, the tote bag she uses for volunteer days. He watches her move through the house, the efficient grace of a woman who knows exactly where she's going and what she's doing when she gets there.

"Food pantry today?" he asks.

"Until one or two, probably. The Hendersons are bringing a truck full of donations from the beach churches, so we'll be sorting and stocking all morning." She pauses at the door, looking back at him. "There's leftover quiche in the fridge if you get hungry. And don't forget: pages."

"Pages," he repeats.

She smiles at him, that particular smile, the one that says *I love you* and *I believe in you* and *you're going to make me proud if you just sit down and do the work*, and then she's gone. The door closes. A moment later, her car starts in the driveway, pulls out, fades into the distance.

The house is silent.

He stands in the kitchen, coffee cooling in his hands, and listens to the emptiness.

* * *

The dog finds him before he finds the dog.

A cold nose against his calf, a heavy tail thumping the cabinet. He looks down. Duke is sitting at his feet, watching him with that patient, expectant look that means only one thing.

"All right," he says. "All right."

He opens the back door and the lab pushes past him, bounding down the steps and across the lawn toward the water. He watches from the doorway as Duke reaches the shore and begins his morning patrol, nose to the ground, tail high, working the edge of the marsh with the serious dedication of a dog who believes the world's secrets are hidden in the marsh grass.

The bay is calm. The light is strengthening, burning off the thin mist that hangs over the water. A heron stands motionless in the shallows near the dock, watching for movement. Everything is still. Everything is ordinary.

He closes the door and walks to his office.

It's a small room at the back of the house, barely big enough for the desk, the chair, the bookshelf stuffed with paperbacks and research volumes and the accumulated debris of a writing life. But it has the window. That's why he chose it. The window that looks out over the bay, over the dock, over the boat.

He sits down. Opens the laptop. The screen glows to life, and there it is: the document he's been avoiding for three weeks. The outline. The summary. The promise he made to his publisher, the deadline he's already pushed back twice.

The cursor blinks at him.

He stares at the screen. The document is nearly empty: just a title, a few scattered notes, the skeletal beginnings of an idea that never grew flesh. He's tried a dozen approaches. Maybe two dozen. He's written openings and deleted them, sketched characters and abandoned them, built worlds and burned them down. The wastebasket beside his desk is full of crumpled paper, the physical drafts he still makes by hand when he's desperate, the longhand attempts to shake something loose.

Nothing has worked.

He tells himself it's the pressure. The first two books came easy, or easier, anyway. The first one he wrote for himself, late at night after long days on the water, never expecting anyone to read it. The second one he wrote because the first one had found an audience, and the story was already there, waiting. But this one, the third one, the contracted one, the one with real money and real expectations behind it, is supposed to be something. Supposed to prove he's not a fluke.

And he has nothing.

He types a sentence. Reads it. Deletes it.

Types another. Worse than the first. Deletes it.

Outside the window, Duke is still working the marsh edge, tail wagging, oblivious to everything except the scent trail he's following. The heron hasn't moved. The boat rocks gently at the dock, lines creaking, waiting.

The dream surfaces again, unbidden. The stranger's voice: *Try the other side.*

He shakes his head slightly, as if to clear it. Focus. The outline. The book. The work.

But the colors of that unnatural sky keep bleeding through. The stillness of the water. The weight of the words: *The kingdom of the Father is spread out upon the earth, and people do not see it.*

He looks out at the bay. The real bay. The ordinary bay.

And for the first time, he wonders if he's been looking at it wrong his whole life.

The thought unsettles him. He pushes it away. Opens a new document. Tries to start fresh.

An hour passes. Maybe two. The coffee goes cold. The cursor blinks and blinks and blinks.

He writes nothing.

* * *

By noon, he's given up pretending.

He closes the laptop. Pushes back from the desk. Stands at the window for a long moment, watching the light on the water, the boat at the dock, the easy sway of the marsh grass in the breeze.

He tells himself he just needs air. Just needs to clear his head. He'll write this afternoon, after lunch, after he's moved his body and stopped thinking so hard. That's the problem. He's thinking too hard. The words will come if he stops grasping at them.

He knows this isn't true. But he tells himself anyway.

"Duke."

The dog appears from somewhere in the house, tail already wagging, as if he's been waiting all morning for this exact word. He knows what it means. The boat. The water. The good place.

They walk down to the dock together, man and dog, the boards warm under his bare feet. The Pathfinder sits where it always sits, lines tied in the same knots he's tied a thousand times. He unties the bow, then the stern. Duke jumps aboard without being told, taking his usual spot in the bow, nose lifted to catch the wind that isn't there yet.

He steps onto the deck. Starts the motor. Lets it idle while he checks the rods, the tackle, the cooler. Everything where it should be. Everything familiar.

He pulls away from the dock, and the house shrinks behind him. The bay opens up ahead, wide and bright in the midday sun. He feels something in his chest begin to loosen, not the dream, not the weight of it, but something else. The pressure. The expectation. The outline and the deadline and the blinking cursor.

Out here, none of that matters. Out here, he's just a man on a boat, doing what he's done his whole life.

He heads toward the shallows.

* * *

He doesn't go to the place from the dream.

He tells himself it's because the fish won't be there this time of day. The water's too warm, the sun too high. The reds will be holding in the deeper channels, waiting for the afternoon cool before they move back to the flats.

But he knows that's not the real reason.

He's afraid of what he'll find. Or what he won't find.

So he takes the boat south instead, toward the oyster bars near the point, where the water drops off and the channel cuts close to the marsh. Good structure. Reliable fishing. The kind of place he used to bring clients when they wanted to catch something without working too hard for it.

Duke lies in the bow, tongue out, happy. The wind picks up as they move, ruffling his fur, carrying the salt smell of the open sound. The dog doesn't care about dreams or deadlines. The dog only knows this: the boat is moving, the water is wide, and his person is here.

Lem envies the simplicity of it.

The oyster bars come into view: dark clusters breaking the surface, the water around them rippled with current. He cuts the motor and lets the trolling motor take over, easing the boat along the edge of the drop-off. The depth finder shows three feet, then eight, then four feet. Structure below. Fish holding in the shadows.

He picks up a rod. Ties on a soft plastic: chartreuse, the color of redfish food. Casts toward the oysters and lets it sink.

The first fish hits before the lure reaches bottom.

He sets the hook by instinct, feels the weight and the fight, the living pull that travels up through his hands. The fish runs toward the structure; he turns it, works it back, keeps the pressure steady. Duke lifts his head, watching. The fish surfaces, a red, maybe twenty-four inches, copper-bright in the sun, and he lands it, hoists it for a moment, admires the spot near the tail.

"Thank you, God," he murmurs.

The words come without thought. The way they always have.

He releases the fish and watches it vanish into the dark water. Casts again.

The afternoon passes like this. Cast, retrieve, hookset, fight. He catches three more reds before he finds the school: a pod of them working the edge of the channel, feeding hard in the current. He loses count after that. Catch and release, catch and release, the rhythm of it emptying his mind the way nothing else can.

But he keeps three. Three big ones, pushing twenty-eight inches each, heavy and bright. Enough for dinner. Enough to bring something home.

The sun is dropping toward the marsh when he finally stops. His arms are tired. His back aches. Duke is asleep in the bow, paws twitching in some dog dream of his own.

He stows the rods. Starts the motor. Turns the boat toward home.

The dream doesn't surface again until he's halfway back. Then it rises, unbidden, the colors, the stillness, the stranger's voice, and he realizes he hasn't thought about it for hours. The fishing pushed it down. The work of the body silenced the noise of the mind.

But it's still there. Waiting.

He wonders if it will come again tonight.

He's afraid of it. And he wants it.

* * *

The dock appears ahead, the house rising behind it, the familiar shape of home. He brings the boat in slowly, cuts the motor, lets the momentum carry him the last few feet. Duke wakes and jumps onto the dock before the boat has fully stopped, shaking himself, ready for dinner.

He ties the lines. Unloads the cooler with the three reds inside. Carries it to the fish cleaning table at the end of the dock: the weathered wooden surface he's used for twenty years, the same knife, the same hose, the same motions.

He lays out the first fish and begins.

The knife moves without thought. Scale, gut, fillet, flip, repeat. The work of hands that know what they're doing. The bay stretches out beside him, golden now in the late light, the sun sitting low over the marsh. Duke lies at the end of the dock, watching the water, ears pricked for the sound of mullet jumping.

He's halfway through the second fish when he hears her footsteps.

He doesn't look up. He knows the rhythm of her walk on these boards: the particular sound of her shoes, the pace of her stride. She's been home for a while, probably. Watching from the house. Waiting to see if he'd come inside.

She stops beside the cleaning table. He glances up just long enough to see her taking in the scene: the fish, the knife, his hands working, the evidence of a full day on the water.

"Three reds," she says. There's warmth in her voice, but something else too. "Looks like someone had a productive day."

He allows himself a small smile. "Thought I'd clean them for dinner."

She doesn't say anything for a moment. He keeps working: the knife, the flesh, the neat fillets piling up on the board.

"You know we have a freezer full already."

She says it lightly. Lovingly, even. But the truth is there, underneath: they have plenty of fish. They didn't need more. They needed something else.

He nods without answering. Starts on the third fish.

The silence stretches. The water laps at the dock pilings. A gull cries somewhere over the marsh.

"How's the outline coming?"

He feels the question land in his chest. His hands keep moving: the knife, the scales, the familiar work. But slower now. Distracted.

He doesn't look up.

He doesn't answer.

The silence holds. He can feel her watching him, waiting. The question hanging in the air between them like something fragile, something that will break if either of them touches it.

She doesn't push. Not yet. She knows him too well for that.

But she knows. He can feel it. She knows he didn't write. Knows he fled. Knows something is wrong that he's not telling her.

"Dinner in an hour?" she finally says, her voice careful.

He nods.

She stands there a moment longer. Then her hand touches his shoulder, a brief, light pressure, and she turns and walks back toward the house.

He listens to her footsteps fade. The screen door opens and closes.

He's alone again.

He finishes the last fish. Rinses the fillets. Coils the hose. Wipes down the knife.

The sun touches the marsh and begins to sink. The light goes golden, then amber, then the deep rose of evening.

He stands at the end of the dock, fillets in hand, and watches the darkness come.

Somewhere out there, past the dock, past the channel, past the oyster bars, is the shallow bay near the marsh edge. The place from the dream. He didn't go there today. He was afraid.

But tonight, when he closes his eyes, he wonders if it will come to him.

He wonders if *he* will come.

He walks back toward the house, Duke at his heels, the weight of the dream still sitting in his chest where the words should be.

* * *

Chapter Three

The Child on the Shore

He falls asleep without meaning to.

One moment he's lying in bed, staring at the ceiling, Beth's breathing slow and steady beside him. The next moment he's somewhere else.

The sound reaches him first. Not waves. Something higher, more insistent. A rising and falling drone that seems to come from everywhere at once, filling the air like heat made audible.

Cicadas.

He opens his eyes.

He's standing on a beach. Shallow water stretches out before him, so clear it barely looks like water at all, just a thin shimmer over sand, rippling slightly in the late afternoon light. The sun is low, dropping toward the mainland across the sound, turning everything gold.

He knows this place.

Shackleford Banks. The sound side, where the water goes calm and the shore curves gently toward the maritime forest. He's anchored here a hundred times, waded these shallows, watched the sun set over the distant treeline while the cicadas sang their endless summer song.

But something is different.

The light is too rich. Too saturated. The colors deeper than they should be: the green of the forest almost glowing, the gold of the sand almost burning. And the cicadas are louder than he's ever heard them, their chorus swelling and falling in waves that seem to match his heartbeat.

He looks around. The beach is empty.

No. Not empty.

A child.

Maybe fifty yards down the shore, sitting in the shallows where the water is only inches deep. A boy, eight or nine years old, barefoot, wearing shorts and a faded shirt. He's bent over something in the sand, his hands working, completely absorbed.

Lem doesn't remember deciding to walk toward him. But he's walking. His feet are bare (when did he take off his shoes?) and the sand is warm beneath them, the water blood-warm when he steps into the shallows. Each step sends small ripples outward, breaking the mirror surface, and he watches them spread and fade as he approaches.

The child doesn't look up.

He's building something. Not a castle exactly. Something more intricate. Arches of wet sand that curve impossibly, defying gravity. Towers so thin they shouldn't stand, yet they do. The structure rises from the shallows like something dreamed rather than built, held together by laws that don't apply to ordinary sand on ordinary beaches.

Lem stops a few feet away. Watches.

The child scoops water from the shallows and pours it over the structure. The sand darkens, and instead of slumping, it holds. Strengthens. As if the water is feeding it rather than eroding it.

A small wave rolls in, the tide breathing the way it does, and Lem braces for the structure to collapse.

But the wave passes *around* it. Parts like a stream around a stone, leaving the unnatural arches untouched. The water reaches Lem's ankles, wets the hem of his clothes, then withdraws. But it never touches the child's creation. Not once.

The child doesn't seem to notice the miracle. He just keeps working. Scooping. Shaping. Building.

The cicadas swell. The light deepens.

Lem feels something stir in his chest, a sensation he can't name. Not sadness, exactly. Not nostalgia. Something older than both. A kind of ache, like homesickness for a place he's never been. Or a place he's been and forgotten.

He used to do this. He remembers suddenly, not the memory itself but the feeling of the memory. Sitting in the shallows as a boy. Building things that didn't matter. Watching them wash away. Building again. Hours passing without weight. No purpose. No product. Just the sand and the water and his hands.

When did he stop?

The child looks up.

His face is ordinary. Sun-browned, round-cheeked, young. But his eyes: his eyes are not a child's eyes. They hold centuries. Not weariness, not age exactly, but *depth*. As if this boy has watched civilizations rise and fall, has seen every sandcastle ever built and every tide that claimed them. Still and deep, like water that doesn't show its bottom. Ancient eyes in a young face.

"You used to know how to do this," the child says.

The words land softly. No accusation. Just observation. Fact.

Lem opens his mouth to respond, but nothing comes. His throat feels tight.

The child returns to his work. Scooping. Shaping. The structure rises higher under his hands, more elaborate, more impossible.

"When did it become work?"

The question hangs in the air, mixing with the drone of the cicadas.

Lem thinks of the outline. The deadline. The laptop open on his desk, the cursor blinking. The crumpled pages in the wastebasket. He thinks of the way he used to write, late at night after guiding, the words pouring out because they wanted to, because the story was there and needed telling. No contract. No expectation. No one waiting.

When did that change?

He can't remember. It happened so gradually. The first book found readers, and suddenly there was an audience. The second book had a publisher, and suddenly there was a deadline. The thing he loved became the thing he owed. The joy became obligation. And somewhere in that transition, something essential was lost.

He kneels.

The sand beneath his knees is warm. Not sun-warm. Something deeper. Warm like skin. Warm like a living body. He feels it through his clothes, a heat that seems to pulse faintly, as if the beach itself has a heartbeat.

The water is warm around his legs, soaking through his clothes. He doesn't care. He reaches out and begins to help, scooping sand, adding it to the structure, shaping it with hands that feel clumsy and too large beside the child's.

But his sand won't hold. The arches he tries to build collapse. The towers he raises slump and fall. A wave rolls in, the same tide that parted around the child's creation, and washes his work away entirely, leaving only smooth wet sand where his contribution had been.

The child's structure stands untouched. Growing. Unnaturally.

They work together in silence. The cicadas sing. The light turns from gold to amber.

The child speaks again without looking up.

"You made them two things."

Lem's hands stop moving.

"They were supposed to be one."

The words sink into him like stones dropped in still water. He feels them land somewhere deep, somewhere below thought, in the place where truth lives before language finds it.

You made them two things.

Work and joy. Duty and love. The writing he owes and the writing he wants. The life he lives to earn money and the life he lives to be alive. He separated them. He built a wall down the middle of his days and put obligation on one side and meaning on the other. And now he wonders why he feels so hollow. Why the words won't come. Why even catching fish feels like something to prove rather than something to experience.

They were supposed to be one.

He thinks of the man on the boat. The kingdom spread out upon the earth. Is this what it means? Not somewhere else, not later, but *here*: in the doing, in the building, in the work that is also play, in the life that refuses to be divided?

He thinks of Captain Roy. The way he used to come off the boat tired but whole. The way work and life were the same thing for him, not because the work was easy, but because it was his. The fishing wasn't what he did to afford his real life. The fishing was the life. The two were one.

Lem had that once. On the water, guiding. At the desk, writing his first book. The two were one and he didn't even know it. He didn't know it was rare. He didn't know it could be lost.

And then he made them two things.

The child's voice comes again, softer now.

"Why do you hold so tightly to what washes away?"

As if to demonstrate, a small wave rolls in, and this time it takes his work with it. Everything he built, gone in a breath. But the child's structure remains, untouched, beautiful.

The child doesn't flinch. Doesn't mourn. Just watches the water settle, then begins again.

Lem feels tears on his face. He doesn't know when he started crying.

Everything washes away. The sandcastle. The outline. The books. The career. The deadline. The fear. The striving. The desperate grip on things that won't stay. It all washes away, and the only question is whether you spend your life fighting the tide or building anyway, building because the building is the point, because the doing is the gift, because the wave was never the enemy.

Unless you become like children, he thinks. The old words, rising unbidden. *You will never enter the kingdom.*

Is this what that means? Not innocence. Not naivety. But this: the ability to build without grasping, to create without clutching, to work and play as one thing, the way children do before adults teach them to divide their lives into pieces?

He wipes his face with the back of his hand. The tears keep coming.

The child is still working. Small hands scooping, shaping, smoothing.

Lem watches those hands.

And then he sees.

The scars.

In the center of each palm. Not fresh. Old, healed, the skin puckered and pale against the sun-brown. Small hands, marked. Wounded and healed. Carrying something that happened long ago and far away.

His breath stops.

The child looks up. Those ancient eyes in that young face. That ordinary appearance holding something infinite.

And Lem knows. The way you know your own name. The way you know the sound of your mother's voice. Not belief. Knowledge. Certainty that bypasses the mind entirely.

He reaches out.

His hand moves toward the child's hand, toward the scar, toward the proof...

And he wakes in the dark.

* * *

His arm is outstretched. His fingers grasping at nothing.

The ceiling. The thin spill of streetlight through the blinds. Beth beside him, her breathing unchanged. The house silent except for the hum of the air conditioner, the ordinary sounds of the ordinary night.

His face is wet.

He lies still, his arm slowly lowering to the sheet, and he feels it. His knees. A warmth that shouldn't be there, a heat that lingers as if he'd been kneeling on sun-baked sand, on something alive. He reaches down, touches his kneecaps through his pajamas. Warm. Still warm.

And his hands: he rubs his fingers together and feels the grit. Fine grains, almost nothing, but there. Sand. Between his fingers. In the creases of his palms.

That's not possible.

He lies still, feeling the warmth fade from his knees, feeling the grit that shouldn't exist, and the sobs rise in his chest. He fights them. Swallows them down. Beth is right there. If he wakes her, she'll ask what's wrong, and he doesn't know how to answer. How do you explain that you were just on a beach with a child, building sandcastles, and the child had scars on his hands, and you knew, you knew, who he was?

You don't explain it.

You can't.

He presses his hand over his mouth and lets the tears come silently. His body shaking. The pillow growing damp beneath his head.

The dream is still there. Not fading. Not dissolving into fragments the way dreams do. It sits inside him whole and heavy, every detail vivid: the warmth of the water, the drone of the cicadas, the child's voice asking questions he can't answer.

You made them two things. They were supposed to be one.

He sees the hands again. The scars. The small palms marked with wounds that shouldn't exist on a child.

And he sees his own hand reaching out. The moment of almost-touching. The waking that came like exile.

He lies in the dark for a long time.

Beth sleeps on, undisturbed. She doesn't know. She won't know. He can't tell her this one. The first dream was strange enough, a man on a boat, words about the kingdom. But this? A child with scars? The certainty that keeps rising in him like a tide he can't hold back?

She'll think he's losing his mind.

Maybe he is.

He turns his head and looks at her. The familiar shape of her under the blanket. The curve of her shoulder. The way she sleeps with one hand tucked under her cheek, the way she's slept for thirty years.

He loves her. He loves this life they've built. And he has no idea how to carry what's happening to him without setting it all on fire.

So he says nothing.

He lies in the dark, alone with the dream, alone with the knowledge, alone with the tears drying on his face.

After a while, an hour, maybe more, his breathing slows. His body stops shaking. The weight of the night settles over him, and something like calm arrives. Not peace, exactly. But acceptance. The understanding that whatever this is, he can't outrun it. He can't explain it away. He can only wait, and see, and try to keep living his life while something larger moves beneath the surface.

The child's voice echoes in the silence.

Why do you hold so tightly to what washes away?

He closes his eyes.

He doesn't sleep. But he rests, somewhere at the edge of consciousness, listening to Beth breathe, feeling the hours pass.

When the light finally begins to gray the windows, he gets up quietly. Dresses in the dark. Walks downstairs to the kitchen, to the coffee pot, to the window that looks out over the bay.

The water is flat and silver in the early morning. The dock stretches out toward the boat. The marsh beyond is dark, not yet touched by sun.

Everything looks the same.

Everything is different.

He makes his coffee. Holds the cup without drinking. Watches the light strengthen over the water.

Duke finds him there, the cold nose against his calf, the hopeful eyes. He reaches down and scratches behind the dog's ears, grateful for the simple need, the uncomplicated love.

"I know," he murmurs. "I know."

He lets the dog out. Watches him bound down to the shore, nose working, tail high. The same patrol as every morning. The same routine.

Beth will be up soon. She'll come downstairs and ask how he slept. And he'll say "fine" or "okay" or some other small lie that protects them both from the truth.

Because the truth is too big for this kitchen. Too strange for this morning. Too much for the life they've built together.

He'll keep it to himself. For now. Maybe forever.

But the child's words keep turning in his mind, and he knows they won't let him go.

You made them two things. They were supposed to be one.

He looks out at the water. At the boat. At the marsh where the light is just beginning to touch the marsh grass.

Somewhere out there, south, past the channels, past the shoals, Shackleford lies quiet in the dawn. The beach where the child sat. The shallows where they built together. The place where small hands carried ancient scars.

He'll go back there someday. He knows it the way he knows his own heartbeat.

But not today.

Today he'll drink his coffee. He'll let the dog in. He'll kiss Beth and pretend everything is normal. He'll sit at his desk and stare at the blinking cursor and fail, again, to find the words.

And tonight, when he closes his eyes, he'll wonder if the dreams will come again.

He's afraid of them.

And yet, he wants them.

* * *

Chapter Four

The Marina

Behind him, footsteps on the stairs.

He straightens. Tries to arrange his face into something normal.

Beth enters the kitchen in her robe, her hair still tousled from sleep. She moves to the cabinet, pulls down a mug, pours her coffee. But she doesn't drink it. She stands there, both hands wrapped around the cup, watching him.

"You're up early again," she says.

"Couldn't sleep."

She nods slowly. Takes a sip. Sets the mug down on the counter with a small click.

"That's three nights in a row."

He doesn't answer.

She moves closer. Not touching him. Just close enough that he can smell her shampoo, the familiar scent of her, the life they've built together.

"Talk to me," she says quietly.

He stares at the window. The heron hasn't moved.

"There's nothing to talk about."

"That's not true."

He turns to look at her. She's studying him with an expression he knows well, the one she uses when she's trying to solve a problem, when she's gathering information, when she's deciding how hard to push.

"You haven't written in days," she says. "You're not sleeping. You're barely eating. You disappear for hours and come back with fish we don't need." She pauses. "And you're not *here*. Even when you're standing right in front of me, you're not here."

He wants to tell her. The words are right there, pressing against the inside of his chest like something alive. *I've been dreaming. Not regular dreams. Something else. A man on the boat who told me the kingdom is here. A child on the shore who asked me why I hold on to things that wash away. And I knew them. I knew who they were. And I can't stop thinking about it, and I can't write, and I can't sleep, and I don't know what's happening to me.*

But he can't say it.

Because saying it would make it real. Saying it would mean watching her face change: the concern shifting to confusion, the confusion to fear, the fear to something worse. He's seen it before, in other contexts, with other people. The moment when someone you love decides you've crossed a line they can't follow you across.

He's not ready for that.

So he says: "I'm just tired. The deadline. You know how I get."

She doesn't believe him. He can see it in her eyes: the way they narrow slightly, the way her mouth tightens at the corners.

But she doesn't push.

"Okay," she says.

The word falls between them like a stone into still water.

She picks up her coffee and leaves the room.

He listens to her footsteps on the stairs. The bedroom door closing. The silence that follows.

He stands at the window for a long time, watching the heron, feeling the distance between them widen like a tide pulling out to sea.

* * *

He tries to write.

He owes it to her. He owes it to himself. He owes it to the publisher who believed in him, who gave him money and time and trust. The least he can do is sit at the desk and try.

He opens the laptop. The document appears: the same empty outline, the same scattered notes, the same white space waiting to be filled.

The cursor blinks.

He puts his fingers on the keys.

Nothing comes.

He thinks about his first book: how the words had poured out of him, late nights after long days on the water, the story arriving faster than he could type it. He hadn't known what he was doing. He hadn't cared. He was just a fishing guide with a tale to tell, writing for the joy of it, never imagining anyone would read it.

And then people read it. And then there was a second book, and a publisher, and a contract, and suddenly the thing he loved became the thing he owed.

You made them two things. They were supposed to be one.

He closes his eyes. The child's voice is so clear, so present, it's as if he's standing right beside him.

When he opens his eyes, the cursor is still blinking. The document is still empty.

He types a sentence: *The morning he found the body, the tide was going out.*

He stares at it. Deletes it.

Types another: *She had been dead for three days before anyone noticed she was gone.*

Deletes that too.

The words feel hollow. Mechanical. Like furniture in a room no one lives in.

He pushes back from the desk. His chest is tight. His breath comes short and shallow. The room feels like it's shrinking around him, the walls pressing inward, the ceiling dropping.

He needs to get out.

He grabs his keys and leaves without telling Beth.

* * *

He drives without deciding where he's going.

Through town, past the hardware store and the bait shop and St. Paul's where they were married thirty years ago. Past the waterfront where tourists are already gathering, cameras in hand, searching for the quaint coastal life they saw in magazines. Across the bridge toward the marina, the water sparkling beneath him, the marshes stretching out on either side like green hands reaching for the sea.

He ends up at the docks where Bud Daniels keeps his boat.

He doesn't know why. Except that he does know. Bud has been his closest friend for 35 years, since that summer before Lem's junior year at Chapel Hill, when they'd both worked as deckhands on Captain Roy's shrimp boat. Twelve-hour days in the August heat, hauling nets, sorting catch, learning the water in a way you can only learn it through your hands and your back and your sweat.

Lem had grown up on Sullivan's Island, near the water. But Bud had grown up *on* the water. Downeast to the bone, his people in Beaufort for generations. He'd been born knowing things Lem had to be taught: the tides, the channels, the weather signs written in the clouds. That summer, Bud had taught him more than any book ever could.

And more than that: Bud had given him Beth.

It was Bud who introduced them. Late August, end of the summer, a cookout at someone's fish camp. Beth was back from Meredith College, about to begin teaching elementary school in Beaufort, pretty and sharp and unimpressed by the college boy from South Carolina. Bud had seen something: the way Lem looked at her, maybe, or the way she pretended not to look back. He'd made the introduction, stood back, let it unfold.

Thirty years of marriage. Kate. The life Lem had built on this coast. All of it traced back to Bud Daniels, to a summer on a shrimp boat, to a friendship that had never wavered.

Lem pulls into the gravel lot and parks beside the old white Chevy with the dented tailgate. The truck has been here as long as he can remember, through two engines, three transmissions, and more miles than either of them can count. Bud refuses to let it go. *"She's got character,"* he always says. *"You don't throw away something just because it's been through some things."*

He finds Bud on the dock, kneeling beside his skiff, the old Sea Ox he'd rebuilt himself years ago, nothing fancy, just a solid hull and an outboard that starts when you need it to. The sun is behind him, casting a long shadow across the weathered deck.

"Morning," Bud says without looking up.

"Mornin'."

"You look like hell."

Lem almost smiles. "Thanks."

Bud finishes what he's doing, wipes his hands on a rag, and straightens. He's a big man: broad shoulders, thick hands, a face that's been weathered by decades of sun and salt. Not educated in the way the world usually means. He'd finished high school and gone straight onto the water, never saw the need for anything else. But wise in ways that mattered. He could read the weather, read the water, read people. He'd forgotten more about the marsh and the sound than most men ever learned.

And he loved his friends like family. Fiercer than family, maybe. Lem had seen it over the years: the way Bud showed up when you needed him, never asked for anything in return, never mentioned it after. The kind of loyalty that didn't need to be spoken because it was lived.

Bud had always wondered how Lem, a man "from off," as the Downeast folks said, had become such a good fishing guide. *"You weren't born to it,"* he'd say, shaking his head. *"But damned if you didn't earn it."*

Coming from Bud, that was the highest compliment.

"What's going on with you?" Bud asks now.

"Nothing."

"That's bullshit and you know it."

Lem looks away. Out at the water. The boats rocking gently in their slips, the gulls wheeling overhead, the ordinary morning light falling on everything like a blessing he can't receive.

"Talk to me," Bud says. Not pushing. Just offering. The way he always has.

Lem opens his mouth.

The words are there. The man on the boat. The child on the shore. The scars. The voice. The dreams that feel more real than waking life.

But they won't come out.

How do you tell someone that you think you've seen Christ? How do you say those words out loud without sounding insane? He's spent his whole life in church, Sunday mornings, the familiar rhythms of faith, but this is different. This isn't belief. This is *encounter*. And it doesn't fit into the tidy boxes of religion.

"I'm just tired," he says finally. "Haven't been sleeping."

Bud studies him for a long moment. Those eyes: sharp, knowing, hard to fool.

"You're lying," he says.

"Yeah."

"You want to tell me why?"

Lem shakes his head. "I can't. Not yet."

Bud nods slowly. He doesn't push. He doesn't demand. He just stands there, solid and patient, the way he's stood beside Lem through every hard thing life has thrown at them. Through Lem's father's death. Through

Beth's cancer scare eight years ago. Through the lean years when the charter business nearly failed and the writing hadn't taken off yet. Bud had been there for all of it. Steady as the tide.

"Okay," he says. "But when you're ready, I'm here. You know that."

"I know."

They stand in silence for a while, watching the water. A pelican dives, surfaces with a fish, throws its head back to swallow. The boats creak in their slips. The world goes on, ordinary and indifferent.

"You want to take her out?" Bud asks, nodding toward the Sea Ox. "Just you and me. Burn some gas. Won't even bring the rods. Just ride."

Lem considers it. The two of them on the water, the way they used to do it when they were young and the world was simpler. Bud at the console, Lem leaning against the gunwale, the wind drowning out the need to talk.

It used to fix everything.

But not today.

"Nah," he says. "I should get back."

Bud looks at him a moment longer, then nods. "Alright. But call me if you need anything. I mean it."

"I will."

Lem walks back to his truck, feeling Bud's gaze on his back the whole way. He doesn't turn around. If he turns around, he might say something. And he's not ready.

He's not ready for any of it.

* * *

The drive home takes longer than it should.

He finds himself taking the back roads, the ones that wind through the marshes and along the sound, the ones he used to drive when he was young and had nowhere to be. The windows are down. The air smells like salt and mud and the green growing things that live at the edge of the water.

He thinks about his father.

The old man had been a priest: Episcopal, serving at Holy Cross on Sullivan's Island for twenty years before becoming chaplain at The Citadel. He'd loved the water too, but from a different angle. Sunday afternoons on the dock, teaching young Lem to cast. Evening walks along the shore, pointing out the birds, the clouds, the way the light changed over the marsh. He'd seen God in all of it, had said so, quietly, in his own way.

He'd died ten years ago, cancer eating him from the inside while he refused to stop praying, refused to stop being who he was.

Near the end, he'd said something strange.

They were sitting on the porch, watching the sunset, not talking much. His father's hands were shaking, they always shook by then, and his voice was thin, barely more than a whisper.

"I saw your mother last night," he'd said.

Lem's mother had been dead for fifteen years.

"In a dream?" Lem had asked.

His father had shaken his head slowly. *"No. Not a dream. She was just... there. Standing at the foot of the bed. Smiling at me."*

Lem hadn't known what to say. He'd chalked it up to the morphine, the disease, the mind letting go as the body failed.

But now he wonders.

Now he wonders if his father saw something real. If the veil between worlds had thinned for him the way it seems to be thinning now. If the dead and the divine move closer when we stop gripping so tightly to the life we think we know.

Why do you hold so tightly to what washes away?

He pulls into the driveway and sits there for a moment, hands on the wheel, engine idling.

Beth is standing on the porch.

Arms crossed. Face tight. Not angry. Something worse. She's been waiting for him. And something has happened.

He turns off the engine. Gets out slowly.

"You left without saying anything," she says.

"I know. I'm sorry. I just needed..."

"Your publisher called."

The words stop him cold.

"What?"

"Margaret. She called the house. She wanted to check in on the outline. She said you haven't answered her emails in two weeks." Beth's voice is steady, controlled, but he can hear what's underneath: the humiliation, the confusion, the fear. "I didn't know what to tell her. I didn't even know you'd stopped responding."

He stands there, frozen.

"I told her you were dealing with some personal things," she continues. "I told her you'd call her back today. She said she understood, but..." She trails off, shakes her head. "She's worried about you. I could hear it in her voice."

He should say something. He should explain. But what explanation is there? *I haven't answered because I can't write. I can't write because I'm dreaming of Christ. And I can't tell you about it because you'll think I'm losing my mind.*

"Why didn't you tell me?" she asks. "Why didn't you tell me it had gotten this bad?"

"I didn't want you to worry."

"I'm your wife." Her voice cracks, just slightly. "Worrying about you is part of the job."

He looks at her. This woman he's loved for thirty years. This woman who has stood beside him through every failure, every success, every ordinary day that made up their extraordinary life together. This woman Bud had introduced him to at a fish camp cookout, the best gift anyone had ever given him.

She comes down the porch steps, stops a few feet away from him. Close enough to touch. Too far to reach.

"What is happening to you?" she asks. "And don't tell me you're tired. Don't tell me it's the deadline. Something is wrong. Something has been wrong for days, and you won't let me in."

He wants to. God, he wants to.

But how do you let someone into a room they can't see? How do you share a dream that dissolves the moment you try to speak it?

"I know," he says. "I know something is wrong."

"Then tell me. Please. Tell me what it is."

He looks at her. Opens his mouth.

I've been dreaming of Christ.

The words are right there.

But they won't come.

"I don't know how," he says instead. And it's the truest thing he's said in days.

Her face crumples. Not into tears. She's too strong for that. But something breaks behind her eyes, some last hope that he would let her in.

"Okay," she says quietly. "Okay."

She turns and walks back into the house.

Lem stands in the driveway, alone, listening to the screen door close behind her.

The marsh stretches out beyond the house. The water glimmers in the afternoon light. Somewhere out there, past the channels and the shoals, Shackleford lies quiet under the sun.

He thinks of the child on the shore. The man on the boat. The words that won't leave him.

The kingdom of the Father is spread out upon the earth, and people do not see it.

He sees it now. Or he's beginning to.

But the seeing is costing him everything.

* * *

Chapter Five

The Fisherman's Hands

He doesn't expect to sleep.

The house has gone quiet in the way houses go quiet when the people inside them have stopped talking. Beth is in bed beside him, but the space between them feels wider than the mattress. They said goodnight without saying anything else. She turned off her lamp. He turned off his. The darkness settled over them like a third presence in the room.

He lies there, staring at the ceiling, listening to her breathe.

She's not asleep. He can tell by the rhythm: too shallow, too controlled. She's lying there in the dark, waiting for something. Waiting for him to speak. Waiting for him to explain. Waiting for the man she married to come back from wherever he's gone.

He wants to reach for her. Wants to say something that would bridge the distance. But what words could possibly hold what's happening to him?

He has no words.

So he lies still, and she lies still, and the silence stretches between them like the dark water of the sound at night.

Eventually her breathing changes. Deepens. She's asleep at last, pulled under by exhaustion.

He closes his eyes.

He doesn't expect to sleep.

But sleep comes anyway, rising up like a tide, pulling him under before he knows he's going.

* * *

The smell reaches him first.

Diesel and salt. Fish blood and rust. The sharp, unmistakable scent of a working waterfront, not the marina where the pleasure boats dock, but the other place. The place where the commercial boats tie up. The place where men make their living from the water the way men have done for a thousand years.

He opens his eyes.

He's standing on the dock behind the fish house. He knows this place, knew it, when he was young. That summer before his junior year at Chapel Hill, when he'd worked as a deckhand on Captain Roy's shrimp boat. Twelve-hour days in the August heat, hauling nets alongside Bud Daniels, learning the water in a way his father had never taught him.

His father had taught him other things. The liturgy. The prayers. The ancient rhythms spoken in the sanctuary at Holy Cross on Sullivan's Island, where his father had served before taking on duties as chaplain at the Citadel. His father's hands had held prayer books and communion wafers, had been raised in blessing over the faithful, had broken bread at the altar. Sacred work. Lem had never doubted that. But sacred work done with words, in high places, in clean vestments.

Captain Roy's hands were different.

That summer, Lem had watched those hands, brown and cracked, scarred from decades of work, mend nets, splice rope, gut fish, coil lines. Hands that never stopped moving. Hands that knew the water the way his father's hands knew the Book of Common Prayer.

Two kinds of sacred work. Lem hadn't understood that then. He'd thought he was just earning money, just having an adventure before returning to college. He hadn't known that Captain Roy was teaching him something his father couldn't teach: that the holy lives in labor too, in sweat and salt and the mending of torn things.

He hasn't been to this dock in years. A decade, maybe longer. After Captain Roy passed, there was no reason to come. The world moved on. The old fishermen retired or died. The fish house changed hands, then changed again. The tourists found other places to take their pictures.

But here it is. Exactly as he remembers.

The building rises behind him, corrugated metal stained with age, a single light burning above the loading dock. The water stretches out ahead, black and still, the commercial trawlers rocking gently in their slips. Nets hang drying on the rails. Crab pots are stacked along the dock in towers that lean against each other like old men sharing secrets.

The light is strange. Not dawn, not dusk, something in between. The sky is the color of old pewter, and the air feels thick, held, expectant. The way the air felt on the boat that first morning. The way it felt on the shore with the child.

He is dreaming. He knows it now. Knows the texture of it, the weight.

He looks around.

A man is sitting at the end of the dock on an overturned crate, bent over something in his lap. His back is to Lem, but there's something familiar in the slope of his shoulders, the way he holds himself: patient, unhurried, utterly absorbed in the work of his hands.

Lem's chest tightens.

He knows that posture. He spent a summer watching it. Early mornings on this same dock, waiting while Captain Roy finished the work that always needed finishing. The nets that always needed mending. The traps that always needed repair. The old man had never rushed, never complained, never seemed to notice the heat or the hour. He just worked, steady as the tide, until the work was done.

He walks toward the man. His footsteps make no sound on the weathered boards.

As he gets closer, he sees what the man is doing. Mending a net. The old way: the way nobody does it anymore, with a wooden net needle and twine, fingers moving in the rhythm that commercial fishermen have used for centuries. Loop, pull, knot. Loop, pull, knot. The movements sure and steady, unhurried, almost meditative.

But something is wrong.

The net needle in the man's hands. Lem recognizes it. The worn groove along the side, the notch where the wood cracked and was sanded smooth. It's Captain Roy's needle. The one Bud inherited when the old man died. The one Lem has seen Bud use a hundred times, mending his own nets on the Sea Ox.

Yet here it is, moving through the mesh like it never stopped.

Lem stops a few feet away.

The man doesn't look up.

His hands are weathered, brown and cracked, knuckles swollen with age and labor. Scars crisscross the fingers, pale lines from old cuts, the accumulated wounds of a lifetime on the water. The hands of someone who has never done easy work.

Captain Roy had hands like that. Toward the end, when age was stealing his breath, those hands still wanted to work. Still reached for rope and net and knife, even when his lungs couldn't keep up.

The man on the crate is not Captain Roy. Lem knows this. The shape of the jaw is different. The set of the shoulders. But something in the way he sits, the way his fingers move through the familiar rhythm, it makes Lem's throat tighten with a grief he thought he'd finished carrying years ago.

The water laps against the pilings. A boat creaks in its slip. The single light above the fish house hums faintly, casting a yellow circle on the weathered boards.

"Ya gonna stand there all night?"

The man's voice is low and rough, thick with the old coastal accent: the voice of the men who worked these docks before the tourists came, before the regulations changed, before the world moved on and left them behind.

"Or ya gonna sit down?"

Lem looks around. Another crate sits a few feet away, half-hidden in the shadow of a stack of traps. He pulls it over, the wood scraping against the dock, and sits.

They're an arm's length apart now. The torn net spread between them, pooling on the boards like something alive.

The man keeps working. Loop, pull, knot. He doesn't look up.

Lem watches his hands. The net needle moving through the mesh. The twine pulling tight. The small, patient repairs that will make the net whole again.

Captain Roy used to say that mending was more important than catching. Anyone can catch fish when the net is whole. But the net is never whole for long. The ocean tears at it. The catch strains it. Time and salt and use wear it down. The real work: the work that matters. It is the mending that happens after.

Lem hasn't thought about that in years.

"You know how to do this?" the man asks.

"Used to. Captain Roy taught me. The summer I worked on his boat."

"Long time ago?" The man grunts. His hands keep moving.

"Yeah. Long time."

Lem watches the net needle weave through the torn mesh. In and out. Loop, pull, knot. The rhythm of it is hypnotic, ancient, unchanged across centuries.

"You miss it," the man says.

Lem doesn't answer right away. He's not sure what he's being asked. The mending? The dock? Captain Roy? That summer when everything was simpler?

"Yeah," he says finally. "I do."

The man nods slowly. His hands never stop.

The silence stretches between them, but it's not uncomfortable. It's the silence of men who know how to work alongside each other without filling the air with words. The silence Lem remembers from that summer, sitting on this same dock with Bud, waiting for Captain Roy, watching the boats come in.

After a while, the man reaches into the bucket beside him and pulls out another net needle. Already wound with twine. He holds it out without looking up.

Lem takes it.

The wood is smooth and warm, worn down by years of handling. It fits in his palm the way it used to fit when he was twenty, learning a trade that wasn't his birthright but felt like it anyway.

He finds a tear in the net, a ragged hole the size of his fist, and begins to work. His fingers are clumsy at first. It's been so long. The twine tangles. The knots come out wrong.

But the man doesn't correct him. Doesn't watch. Just keeps working on his own section, patient and steady.

Slowly, Lem's hands remember. The rhythm comes back. Loop, pull, knot. Loop, pull, knot. His shoulders loosen. His breathing slows.

They work in silence.

The light neither brightens nor fades. The water laps at the pilings. The boats creak in their slips. The world feels held, suspended, outside of time.

Lem doesn't know how long they work. Minutes, maybe. Or hours. Time moves differently here, in this place that is and isn't the dock he remembers.

Finally, the man speaks.

"You've been looking for me."

Lem's hands falter. The net needle stops.

"I've been dreaming," he says carefully.

"I know."

The man keeps working. Loop, pull, knot.

"You've been looking in the wrong places, though."

Lem frowns. "What do you mean?"

The man doesn't answer right away. He ties off a knot, examines it, moves to the next tear. His hands never hurrying.

"Where do you go to find me?" he asks.

Lem opens his mouth. Closes it.

"Church," he says finally. "Prayer. The Bible."

The man nods slowly. Still not looking up.

"High places," he says. "Clean places. Places with stained glass and organ music. Places where everything is arranged just right."

The words aren't harsh. They're almost gentle. But they land somewhere deep in Lem's chest.

"Nothing wrong with those places," the man continues. "I'm there too. In the bread your father broke. In the words he spoke over the faithful. In every blessing his hands ever gave."

Lem's breath catches. The man knows about his father. Knows about the sanctuary, the liturgy, the sacred work done in vestments and candlelight.

"Your father knew me," the man says. "Served me his whole life. Every prayer he offered, every sacrament he performed, I was there. I've always been there."

Lem feels tears pricking at his eyes. His father, the priest. The man who'd wanted Lem to follow him into the church, or at least into the Citadel, the family tradition. The man who'd been quietly disappointed when Lem chose Chapel Hill, then Beaufort, then the water instead of the altar.

Had his father known? Had he felt the presence that Lem was only now beginning to feel?

"But you think that's the only place I live," the man continues. "Up there. Somewhere else. Somewhere you have to climb to reach. Somewhere you have to dress up and speak correctly and kneel in the right posture."

He gestures with the net needle, a small motion that takes in the whole dock. The fish house with its rusted walls. The trawlers with their peeling paint. The crab pots and the torn nets and the black water and the smell of diesel and blood.

"I'm here too."

Lem looks around. The ordinary decay of a working waterfront. The unglamorous machinery of men making their living from the sea.

"Your father taught you one kind of sacred work," the man says. "And it was real. It was true. Never doubt that."

He ties off a knot, examines it.

"But Captain Roy taught you another kind. And that was just as real. Just as true."

Lem stares at him. The summer on the shrimp boat. The nets. The labor. The old man's patience as he taught two young men how to mend what was broken.

"Split a piece of driftwood," the man says. "I am there."

Lem goes still.

"Lift a shell from the sand, and you will find me."

The words settle into him like stones dropping into still water. Ripples spreading outward, touching everything.

The man keeps working. Loop, pull, knot.

Lem stares at the net in his hands. The torn mesh. The twine. The work of mending.

He thinks about his father, standing at the altar in his vestments, speaking the words of consecration. And he thinks about Captain Roy, standing on this dock in his rubber boots, teaching a college boy how to make a net whole again.

Two men. Two kinds of sacred work. Both true.

His father had served God in the sanctuary. Captain Roy had served God on the water. And Lem. Lem had been given both. The liturgy and the labor. The prayers and the nets. The high places and the low ones.

"Why did I think I had to choose?" he whispers.

"You didn't have to choose. You just forgot."

The man ties off another knot. His hands pause: the first time they've stopped.

"You thought you'd outgrown this place. Thought the sacred was somewhere else. In the books you read. The words you wrote. The ideas in your head."

He reaches for a rag beside him, stained and gray, the kind of rag that's wiped a thousand hands on a thousand mornings. He runs it over his fingers, cleaning the fish scales and salt from his skin.

"But I never left the docks. Never left the water. Never left the places where people work and sweat and bleed and haul their nets in before dawn."

When he sets the rag down, Lem stares.

The rag is clean. Pristine. As if no hand had ever touched it.

But the man's hands are still weathered, still scarred. The dirt and scale should be on the cloth. It isn't.

Lem's heart beats faster. A quiet miracle. A sign that says *pay attention*.

The man doesn't seem to notice. He picks up his net needle again.

"I was in the sanctuary with your father," he says. "And I was on the boat with Captain Roy. And I was in the words you wrote, and the fish you caught, and the nets you mended. Every act of honest work. Every moment of real attention. Every time you forgot yourself in the doing of something that needed to be done."

He looks up.

And the eyes.

The eyes are the same.

The boat at dawn. The child on the shore. Now the dock behind the fish house.

The same eyes.

"I've been here the whole time," he says. "In both places. In all places. Waiting for you to see."

Lem feels something crack open in his chest. Not breaking. More like a door that's been stuck for years finally swinging free.

He wants to ask a thousand questions. Wants to understand what's happening to him, what it means, what he's supposed to do with it. But only one question rises to the surface. The one that's been burning in him since the first dream.

"Why are you speaking to *me?*"

The man is quiet for a long moment. The water laps at the pilings. The light hums above the fish house. The world waits.

Then he says, simply:

"Because you've been speaking to me your whole life."

Lem's breath stops.

"You just didn't know I was listening."

The words land like a hand on his chest. Firm and gentle at the same time.

Every prayer. Every muttered word of thanks over a fish. Every whispered plea in the dark of his bedroom. Every moment of wordless gratitude for the water and the light and the life he was given. Every time he'd knelt beside his father in the pew and spoken the ancient words. Every time he'd stood on the deck of a boat and felt something vast and holy moving beneath him.

He thought those words fell into silence. Vanished like breath into cold air. He thought no one was listening because no one ever answered.

But someone was listening.

Someone has always been listening.

In the sanctuary and on the dock. In the prayers and in the labor. In every high place and every low one.

Lem feels the tears rising. He doesn't try to stop them.

"I thought..." His voice breaks. "I thought I was alone."

"You were never alone."

"I hear you."

"I've always heard You."

The man sets down his net needle. Straightens slowly. Turns.

The face is weathered. Lined. Ordinary. The face of a man who has spent decades working in the sun and salt and wind.

But the eyes.

The eyes are the same.

Ancient and present at once. Holding depths that shouldn't fit in a human face. Holding something that Lem has no name for, something that makes his whole body tremble with recognition.

I know you.

The thought rises unbidden.

I've always known you.

The man's face is calm. Patient. Full of something that might be called love, if love could be that vast and that intimate at the same time.

Lem's hand moves without his permission. Reaching out. Reaching toward.

And he wakes in the dark, his arm extended, his fingers grasping at nothing.

His face is wet.

Not just tears this time. His whole pillow is soaked, his cheeks streaked, his eyes swollen. He's been weeping in his sleep. Weeping the way you weep at funerals, at births, at the moments that crack you open and remake you.

His body is trembling. Not from cold. From something deeper.

He brings his hand to his face, and smells it. Diesel. Fish. Salt. The smell of the dock, the smell of the net, the smell of the work. Faint but unmistakable, clinging to his skin.

And his fingers, he rubs them together, they're grooved. Faint red lines across the pads, the kind of marks twine leaves when you've been working it for hours.

That can't be real.

But it's there.

Beside him, Beth is sitting up. The lamp is on. She's staring at him, and her face is pale, her eyes wide with something that looks like fear.

"Lem."

Her voice is shaking.

"Lem, you were crying. For a long time. I couldn't wake you. I tried, and you just kept..."

She stops. Swallows.

"You kept saying something. Over and over."

He blinks at her. The room feels too bright, too small. The dream is still inside him, more vivid than the walls around him.

"What did I say?"

She hesitates. Her hands are gripping the blanket so tightly her knuckles are white.

"'I hear you,'" she whispers. "'I hear you. I hear you.' You kept saying it. And reaching for something. And crying."

He closes his eyes.

I hear you.

Not his words to the man on the dock.

The man's words to him.

Somehow, in his sleep, he'd been speaking them back. Receiving them. Confirming them.

I hear you.

I've always heard you.

"Lem." Beth's voice is closer now. Urgent. "What is happening to you? Please. You have to tell me."

He opens his eyes. Looks at her. This woman he has loved for over thirty years. This woman who has stood beside him through everything. This woman who is looking at him now like he's a stranger.

He opens his mouth to tell her.

The man on the boat. The child on the shore. The fisherman on the dock. The eyes that are always the same. The words that won't let him go.

I've been dreaming of Christ.

But the words won't come. Not yet. Not to her.

It's not that he doesn't trust her. It's that the dreams are still too large, too holy, too fragile. Speaking them to someone who wasn't there, someone who didn't see them, didn't feel them, would reduce them somehow. Flatten them into something explainable. Something that could be diagnosed and treated and made to go away.

And he doesn't want them to go away.

He's terrified. And he wants more.

"I don't know how to explain it," he says. And it's the truest thing he can offer right now.

Her face crumples. Not into tears. Not yet, but into something worse. Defeat.

"Okay," she says quietly. "Okay."

She turns off the lamp. Lies back down. Doesn't touch him.

The darkness settles over them again.

They lie there, side by side, two people who have shared a bed for three decades but are now separated by something neither of them can name.

He listens to her breathing. Waiting for it to slow. Waiting for her to sleep.

But she doesn't sleep.

Neither does he.

The first gray light is touching the windows when Beth finally speaks.

"I'm going to call Kate."

Lem doesn't answer.

"I'm going to ask her to come home. Today."

He stares at the ceiling. The water stain in the corner that he keeps meaning to fix. The hairline crack that runs from the window to the light fixture.

"Okay," he says.

He hears her get up. Pull on her robe. Pad out of the room.

Her footsteps in the hall. The creak of the stairs. Then, faintly, her voice, low, trying not to carry, but he can hear the fear in it even from here.

"Katie, honey. I'm sorry to call so early. I need you to come home. Something's wrong with your father. I don't know what. He won't talk to me. He just... Katie, please. I need you."

The words drift up through the floorboards, and Lem closes his eyes.

He should feel guilty. He's frightening the people he loves. He's failing them in ways he doesn't know how to fix.

But the dream is still with him, whole and heavy and real. The dock. The net. The man's voice.

You've been speaking to me your whole life. You just didn't know I was listening.

Every prayer. Every word. Every breath of gratitude or longing or despair.

Heard.

All of it.

Always.

In the sanctuary and on the dock. In his father's church and on Captain Roy's boat. In every high place and every low one.

He lies in bed, watching the light grow stronger, and thinks about the church service this morning. The liturgy they'll speak. The prayers they'll offer. The hymns they'll sing.

He's said those words a thousand times. The Lord's Prayer. The Nicene Creed. The Confession of Sin. He's spoken them so often they've become background noise, syllables worn smooth by repetition, meaning drained out by habit.

But now.

Now he knows someone is listening.

Chapter Six

Sunday

The drive to church is quiet.

Lem sits in the passenger seat, watching the familiar roads slide past, the turn at the old hardware store, the stretch along the waterfront, the oak-lined street that leads to St. Paul's. Beth drives the way she always drives on Sunday mornings: carefully, unhurried, her hands at ten and two.

She hasn't spoken since they got in the car.

He hasn't either.

The silence between them is different now. Heavier. It's not the comfortable quiet of a long marriage, two people who don't need to fill every moment with words. It's the silence of things unsaid. Things that can't be said. A wall neither of them knows how to climb.

Lem looks out the window. The morning is bright, the sky a hard blue, the kind of December day that tricks you into thinking spring is closer than it is. Families are walking toward the church, dressed in their Sunday clothes. Children run ahead on the sidewalk. Everything looks normal.

Everything feels wrong.

He slept maybe an hour after the dream. Maybe less. His body is heavy with exhaustion, but his mind won't quiet. The dock keeps rising behind his eyes. The net. The man's hands. The voice.

You've been speaking to me your whole life. You just didn't know I was listening.

He's about to walk into a building full of people speaking to God. Prayers and hymns and responses, rising up from the pews the way they've risen for centuries. And now he knows, *knows* that every word lands somewhere. That the silence they speak into is not silence at all.

Beth pulls into the parking lot. Finds their usual spot. Turns off the engine.

She sits there a moment, hands still on the wheel, staring straight ahead.

"Lem."

He waits.

"Whatever is happening to you..." She stops. Starts again. "I'm scared. I need you to know that. I'm scared, and I don't know how to help you, and I need you to let me in."

He turns to look at her. Her profile against the window. The lines around her eyes that weren't there when they married. The set of her jaw, tight with the effort of holding herself together.

He loves her. He has loved her for thirty years. And he is causing her pain, and he doesn't know how to stop.

"I know," he says. "I'm sorry."

"Don't be sorry. Just... talk to me. Please."

He opens his mouth. The words are there, pressing against his chest. *I've been dreaming of Christ. He comes to me at night. He speaks to me. And I know it sounds crazy, but it's real, Beth. It's more real than anything I've ever experienced.*

But the words won't come. Not here. Not now. Not in a church parking lot with families streaming past and the bells about to ring.

"After," he says. "After the service. I'll try."

She looks at him. Searches his face for something: hope, maybe, or reassurance. He doesn't know if she finds it.

"Okay," she says quietly.

They get out of the car. Walk toward the church. Side by side, but not touching.

* * *

St. Paul's has only one set of doors.

Lem has entered them a thousand times, more than a thousand, across thirty years of Sundays. The doors are old, heavy, the wood dark with age. It opens onto the narthex, and beyond that, the nave, and beyond that, the altar where the mystery happens.

One set of doors in. One set of doors out. No slipping away unnoticed. No quiet exit. You enter through those doors, and when the service ends, you leave through them, past the priest, past the handshake, past the weekly ritual that seals the covenant between shepherd and flock.

Lem has never minded. The doorway is part of it. The way the pew is part of it.

St. Paul's is a small Episcopal church, white clapboard with a modest steeple, built in the 1850s by the families who first settled this part of the coast. Lem and Beth have been coming here since they married. Thirty years of Sundays, give or take. They were married in this church. Kate was baptized here, his father's weathered hands pouring the water while Lem held his infant daughter and heard the words that would shape the rest of his life. They've sat through Christmas pageants and Easter vigils and ordinary Sundays beyond counting.

The building knows him. The worn wooden pews, the stained glass windows with their faded blues and reds, the particular creak of the floorboards near the baptismal font. This place has been the architecture of his faith for over three decades: steady, familiar, unchanging.

But today it feels different.

Today it feels like he's seeing it for the first time.

They enter through the doorway and make their way down the aisle on the left.

And there it is. Third from the back, left side. *His* pew.

Not "a" pew. Not a favorite spot. *His.* The place he has sat every Sunday for thirty years, since he and Beth first walked into this church as newlyweds and chose their spot: third from the back, left side, close enough to see, far enough to slip out if Kate fussed.

The wood is worn smooth where his hand rests on the edge. There's a small groove, barely visible, but he knows it's there, where his fingers have traced the same path week after week, year after year. The hymnal rack in front of him has a slight wobble; he noticed it fifteen years ago and never reported it, because it's part of the pew now, part of *his* pew, and he doesn't want anyone to fix it.

Some men build altars of stone. Lem built his of presence.

This is where he sat when his father died. This is where he sat when Kate was baptized, watching his father pour water over her head, hearing the words that would echo through the rest of his life: *You are responsible for the Christian upbringing of this child.* This is where he sat when the fish were biting and when they weren't, when the writing was going well and when it wasn't, when he had something to offer God and when he came empty.

The pew doesn't care. The pew just holds him.

Beth slides in first. Lem follows. His hand finds the worn edge, the familiar groove. His body settles into the shape it's made over decades.

He is here. He is present. Whatever else is happening, the dreams, the visitors, the words that won't let him go, he is here, in his place, doing what he has always done.

He looks around. The sanctuary is filling up: the usual Sunday crowd, maybe fifty people, faces he's known for years. Margaret Wilson, who runs the food pantry with Beth. Frank and Dottie Simmons, who lost their son in Afghanistan and have never missed a Sunday since. The Peterson kids, fidgeting in the front row while their mother tries to quiet them.

Ordinary people. Ordinary lives. All of them about to speak words into the silence.

All of them heard.

The organ begins: a prelude, something by Bach, the notes rising and falling in the high-ceilinged space. Lem feels the music in his chest. It's always been beautiful to him, but today it's almost unbearable. Each note seems to carry weight, seems to mean something beyond itself.

He grips the edge of the pew.

Beth glances at him. He can feel her attention, her worry. He doesn't look at her.

The processional begins. The acolytes first, carrying the cross and the candles, their white robes bright against the dark wood of the aisle. Then the choir: eight voices, mostly older women, singing the opening hymn. And finally Father John, vested in purple, the color of Advent, his face composed in the expression Lem has seen a thousand Sundays: calm, welcoming, priestly.

The congregation rises. Lem rises with them. His hymnal is open in his hands, but he's not looking at the words. He knows them by heart. Everyone knows them by heart.

"Holy, holy, holy, Lord God Almighty..."

The voices rise around him. Fifty people, singing. The words ascending through the old wooden rafters, through the roof, into the bright December sky.

"Early in the morning our song shall rise to thee..."

Lem's throat tightens. His hands are trembling on the hymnal.

These words. He's sung them hundreds of times. They've always been beautiful, in an abstract way: poetry about God, metaphor and music. But now.

Now he hears them differently.

Our song shall rise to thee.

Rise to *whom?* To what? To the empty sky? To a concept? To a theological abstraction?

No.

To *him.* To the one on the boat. The one on the shore. The one at the dock with the net and the ancient eyes.

You've been speaking to me your whole life.

The hymn continues. Lem's voice has stopped. He can't sing. He can only stand there, holding the hymnal, feeling the words wash over him.

Beside him, Beth is singing. Her voice is steady, familiar. She doesn't notice he's stopped. Or maybe she does and is pretending not to.

The hymn ends. The congregation sits. Father John moves to the altar, raises his hands.

"The Lord be with you."

"And also with you," the congregation responds.

Lem mouths the words. No sound comes out.

Father John begins the collect: the opening prayer, the words that gather the congregation's intentions and lift them up. His voice is measured, practiced, the voice of a man who has spoken these words so many times they've become automatic.

"Almighty God, to you all hearts are open, all desires known, and from you no secrets are hid..."

Lem closes his eyes.

All hearts are open. All desires known. No secrets are hid.

He used to think those words were metaphor. A way of speaking about God's omniscience, a theological concept wrapped in poetry.

But now he knows they're literal.

You just didn't know I was listening.

Every secret. Every desire. Every prayer he's whispered in the dark, wondering if God would hear.

His eyes are stinging. He blinks hard. He will not cry. Not here. Not in front of all these people.

The first reading begins. Someone from the congregation, Margaret Wilson, he realizes, stands at the lectern and reads from Isaiah. The prophet's voice, preserved across millennia, speaking of comfort and promise.

"Comfort, comfort my people, says your God. Speak tenderly to Jerusalem, and cry to her that her warfare is ended, that her iniquity is pardoned..."

The words land in him like stones. Comfort. Pardon. An end to warfare.

He thinks of his own warfare: the battle with the blank page, the distance from his wife, the fear that he's losing his mind. The dreams that terrify him and draw him in equal measure.

Is this comfort? Is this pardon?

Or is this the beginning of something that will cost him everything?

The reading ends. The congregation responds: "Thanks be to God."

Lem's lips move. No sound.

The psalm is sung: the choir leading, the congregation following. More words about God's faithfulness, God's presence, God's enduring love. Lem tries to follow along, but the words blur on the page. He's not reading anymore. He's just standing there, letting the music wash over him, feeling something build in his chest that he can't name and can't stop.

The second reading. Paul's letter to the Corinthians. Something about love. The words are famous, *love is patient, love is kind* and Lem has heard them at weddings and funerals and ordinary Sundays beyond counting.

But today they sound different.

Love bears all things, believes all things, hopes all things, endures all things.

He thinks of Beth. The way she's stood beside him for thirty years. The way she's standing beside him now, even though he's shut her out, even though he can't explain what's happening to him.

She's bearing this. She's enduring.

And he's giving her nothing.

The reading ends. The congregation stands for the Gospel.

Father John moves to the center of the aisle, the Book of the Gospels held high. The acolytes flank him with candles. The congregation turns to face him.

"The Holy Gospel of our Lord Jesus Christ according to Luke."

"Glory to you, Lord Christ."

Lem's heart is pounding. He doesn't know why. It's just the Gospel reading, the same thing that happens every Sunday. But something in him knows, *knows* that whatever comes next is going to break him.

Father John begins to read.

"Once Jesus was asked by the Pharisees when the kingdom of God was coming, and he answered, 'The kingdom of God is not coming with things that can be observed; nor will they say, "Look, here it is!" or "There it is!" For, in fact, the kingdom of God is within you.'"

Lem stops breathing.

The kingdom of God is within you.

He hears it in Father John's voice: measured, practiced, unremarkable.

And beneath it, he hears another voice.

The kingdom of the Father is spread out upon the earth, and people do not see it.

The boat at dawn. The stranger beside him. The first dream.

The same teaching. The same truth. Separated by two thousand years, but the same.

His knees buckle slightly. He grabs the pew in front of him to steady himself.

Father John continues reading. Something about the Son of Man, about the days of Noah, about being ready. But Lem isn't hearing it anymore. He's back on the boat, the impossible colors of the sky, the stillness of the water, the man's voice low and certain.

The kingdom is not coming. The kingdom is here. The kingdom is now.

And then, suddenly, without warning, the church around him *shifts*.

It's not a vision, exactly. It's more like a veil being lifted. A layer of the ordinary peeled back to reveal what was always there underneath.

He looks at Father John, standing in the aisle with the Gospel book, and he sees, just for an instant, something else. A presence. A light. The same eyes that have met him in every dream, looking out from behind the priest's familiar face.

Then it's gone. Father John is just Father John again, finishing the reading, closing the book.

"The Gospel of the Lord."

"Praise to you, Lord Christ."

Lem's face is wet.

He reaches up, touches his cheek. Tears. He didn't feel them start. Didn't feel them fall. But they're there, streaming down his face, dripping onto his shirt.

Beth is staring at him. Her eyes wide. Her hand reaching for his arm.

"Lem? Lem, are you..."

He can't answer. He can't speak. He can only stand there, weeping, as the congregation sits down for the sermon and the world continues on as if nothing has happened.

* * *

Father John ascends to the pulpit.

He arranges his notes. Adjusts the microphone. Looks out at the congregation with the warm, practiced expression of a man about to deliver a sermon he's given many times before.

And then his eyes find Lem.

It's a glance at first: the kind of glance a priest makes naturally, scanning the pews, connecting with his flock. But something makes him stop. Something in Lem's face, in the tears still falling, in the way he's gripping the pew like a man trying not to drown.

Father John's expression flickers. Just for a moment. Something moves behind his eyes: confusion, maybe. Or recognition. Or something else entirely.

He looks away. Clears his throat. Begins the sermon.

But his voice is different now. Slightly unsteady. And his eyes keep returning to Lem: quick glances, almost involuntary, as if he can't help himself.

Lem barely hears the sermon. The words wash over him, something about the kingdom, about waiting, about hope, but he can't follow them. He's too far gone, too deep inside whatever is happening to him.

The tears have slowed, but they haven't stopped. Beth is holding his hand now, gripping it tight, her own face pale with worry. He can feel her fear through her fingers, the desperate pressure of a woman trying to hold onto something that's slipping away.

He squeezes back. It's all he can offer.

The sermon ends. The congregation stands for the Nicene Creed.

"We believe in one God, the Father, the Almighty, maker of heaven and earth, of all that is, seen and unseen..."

Fifty voices, speaking together. Words written by councils of bishops sixteen centuries ago, preserved and repeated and passed down through generations.

And now Lem understands.

These aren't just words. They never were. Every Sunday, in churches all over the world, people stand and speak these ancient phrases, and every syllable is heard. Every voice lands somewhere. The faith of millions, rising up like incense, received by the one who was and is and is to come.

He's weeping again. He can't help it. The words are too heavy, too real. He mouths them without sound, his lips moving through the familiar phrases while the tears stream down his face.

"...We believe in one Lord, Jesus Christ, the only Son of God, eternally begotten of the Father, God from God, Light from Light, true God from true God..."

Light from Light.

He sees it now. The light in the dreams. The light behind the eyes. The light that shines through every form: the stranger on the boat, the child on the shore, the fisherman at the dock.

Light from Light.

"...For us and for our salvation he came down from heaven: by the power of the Holy Spirit he became incarnate from the Virgin Mary, and was made man..."

Made man. Became flesh. Walked the earth in a body that could hunger and thirst and weep.

A body that could dream.

"...For our sake he was crucified under Pontius Pilate; he suffered death and was buried..."

The child's hands. The scars in the small palms.

Lem closes his eyes. The image is there, vivid as the moment he saw it. Those hands, building sandcastles in the shallows. Those ancient wounds, still visible on a child's skin.

"...On the third day he rose again in accordance with the Scriptures; he ascended into heaven and is seated at the right hand of the Father..."

Ascended into heaven.

But also here. On the boat. On the shore. On the dock. In this church. In this moment.

Not gone. Not far away. *Here.*

"...He will come again in glory to judge the living and the dead, and his kingdom will have no end."

He will come again.

Lem opens his eyes. Looks up at the altar, at the cross, at the stained glass window where Christ stands with arms outstretched.

He's not coming. He's already here. He never left.

The creed ends. The congregation sits for the prayers of the people.

A woman stands at the lectern, someone Lem knows slightly, a teacher at the elementary school, and begins to lead the prayers. The familiar pattern: she speaks a petition, the congregation responds.

"For the peace of the world, and for the welfare of the holy Church of God, let us pray to the Lord."

"Lord, have mercy."

Fifty voices. One response. The words rising up.

Heard.

"For all who suffer and all who mourn, that they may know the comfort of God's presence, let us pray to the Lord."

"Lord, have mercy."

All who suffer. All who mourn.

Lem thinks of Beth, sitting beside him, her hand still gripping his. Suffering. Mourning something she can't name: the husband she knew, the life they had, the certainty that's crumbling beneath her feet.

"Lord, have mercy," he whispers. The first words he's spoken aloud since the service began.

Beth looks at him. Her eyes are wet now too.

The prayers continue. For the sick. For the dying. For those who have died. For the church and its leaders. For the nation and all who govern.

Each petition a voice lifted. Each response a collective cry.

And all of it heard. Every word. Every plea.

Lem is shaking now. Not from cold. Not from fear. From the weight of it: the sheer, impossible weight of being in a room full of people speaking to God, and knowing, *knowing* that God is listening.

The prayers end. The peace is exchanged.

"The peace of the Lord be always with you."

"And also with you."

The congregation rises, turns, begins the familiar ritual of greeting one another. Handshakes and embraces, murmured blessings, the human warmth of a community at prayer.

Beth turns to Lem. Looks at him. Her face is streaked with tears she doesn't seem to know she's crying.

"Peace," she whispers.

He takes her hands. Both of them. Holds them between his own.

"Peace," he says. "I love you."

She breaks. Just for a moment. Her face crumpling, a sob escaping before she can stop it. Then she pulls herself together, wipes her eyes with the back of her hand, nods.

"I love you too," she says. "Whatever this is. I love you too."

They turn to greet the others around them. Handshakes. Murmured words. The ordinary ritual that suddenly feels sacred.

Because everything is sacred now.

Everything has always been sacred.

He just couldn't see it before.

* * *

The Eucharist begins.

Father John stands at the altar, the bread and wine before him. The ancient words, spoken in the same cadence they've been spoken for two thousand years.

"The Lord be with you."

"And also with you."

"Lift up your hearts."

"We lift them to the Lord."

"Let us give thanks to the Lord our God."

"It is right to give him thanks and praise."

Lem listens to the words. The story of the last supper, the night before he died. *Take, eat: This is my Body, which is given for you. Do this for the remembrance of me.*

Remembrance.

But it's not just remembrance anymore. It's not just a ritual, a symbol, a reenactment of something that happened long ago.

He's here. In this room. In this bread. In this wine.

The same one who sat on the boat. Who built sandcastles on the shore. Who mended nets on the dock.

Do this for the remembrance of me.

Because I'm here. I'm always here. Even when you forget. Even when you go through the motions without feeling. I'm here.

The congregation moves forward for communion. Row by row, they leave their pews and process toward the altar rail, hands outstretched to receive.

Lem and Beth join the line. He walks slowly, his legs unsteady, his heart pounding. The tears have dried on his face, but he can feel them: the salt on his skin, the tightness around his eyes.

He kneels at the rail. The wood is hard under his forearms. The altar is before him, draped in purple, the candles flickering.

Father John moves down the line, the bread in his hands.

"The Body of Christ, the bread of heaven."

He places a wafer in each palm. Person by person. The familiar motion, repeated countless times.

He reaches Lem.

Their eyes meet.

Father John's hand stops, the wafer suspended above Lem's open palm. His face changes: a flicker of confusion, or recognition, or fear. For a long moment, he doesn't move. Just stands there, looking at Lem, looking *into* Lem, as if he's seeing something he can't explain.

Lem looks back. He doesn't know what Father John sees. He only knows what he feels: the presence, vast and intimate, filling the space between them like light.

Father John's hand trembles slightly.

"The Body of Christ," he says. His voice is hoarse. "The bread of heaven."

He places the wafer in Lem's palm.

Their fingers touch. Just for an instant. And in that instant, something passes between them: a current, a knowing, a recognition neither can name.

Then Father John moves on. The chalice bearer follows with the wine. The ritual continues.

But Lem sees it: the way Father John's hands shake as he finishes the communion. The way his eyes keep darting back toward the spot where Lem kneels. The way his face has gone pale against the vestments.

He felt it too.

Lem bows his head. Places the bread on his tongue. Receives the wine.

This is my body. This is my blood.

And it is. It truly is.

* * *

The service ends.

The final hymn. The dismissal. Father John's voice, slightly unsteady now, sending them out into the world.

"Go in peace to love and serve the Lord."

"Thanks be to God."

The congregation rises. The slow shuffle toward the back, toward the single set of double doors, toward Father John waiting in his usual spot. Lem moves with them, Beth's hand on his arm, her grip tight.

He has shaken Father John's hand a thousand times. A thousand Sundays. The same grip, the same eye contact, the same brief exchange that says *I see you, I know you, we are in this together.* It has never meant nothing. Even on the Sundays when Lem was tired, distracted, eager to get home: the handshake meant something. The meeting of eyes meant something.

He is three people away now. Two.

He watches Father John's face. The practiced smile. The pastoral warmth. And beneath it, something else. Something tight. The priest's eyes flick toward Lem, then away. Flick back, then away again. He's tracking Lem's approach the way you track something you dread.

One person ahead. Margaret Wilson, who runs the food pantry with Beth. Father John takes her hand, leans in, says something that makes her smile.

Then she moves on.

And Lem is there.

Father John's hand comes up. Automatic. The muscle memory of ten thousand handshakes. His fingers close around Lem's palm.

But his eyes don't come with them.

Father John is looking at Lem's shoulder. At the door frame. At the bright December morning beyond. Anywhere, everywhere, except Lem's face.

The handshake is weak. Half-hearted. The priest's fingers trembling against Lem's palm: the same tremor Lem felt at the communion rail, when Father John placed the bread in his hands and something passed between them that neither of them could name.

The tremor says: *I know. I felt it. I can't.*

"Lem." Father John's voice is barely a whisper. No *good to see you.* No *God bless.* Just the name, pushed out like a confession.

"Father."

Their hands separate. Father John is already turning, already reaching for the next person in line, his voice warming back into its pastoral register.

"Bill! Good to see you. How's the boat project going?"

Lem steps through the door.

The December air hits his face. Cold. Bright. The world going on.

Beth is beside him. She felt it too. He can tell by the way she's looking at him, the question in her eyes. *What was that? What just happened?*

He doesn't answer. He doesn't have words for it yet.

But he knows what he felt. The priest's hand trembling in his. The eyes that wouldn't meet his own.

Father John *knows.* He felt it at the rail. He felt it again just now.

And he can't bear to look at it.

Beth stops before they reach the car.

"Wait here," she says quietly. "I need to speak to Father John."

Lem looks at her. Her face is set, determined. The fear is still there, but something else too. Resolve.

"Okay," he says.

She squeezes his arm. Turns. Makes her way back through the door, against the flow of the departing congregation.

Lem stands in the parking lot, watching through the doorway.

Father John is still at his post, shaking hands, but the line is thinning. An acolyte is moving through the nave, extinguishing candles. The ordinary cleanup of an ordinary Sunday.

But nothing is ordinary anymore.

Beth approaches him. Speaks quietly. Lem can't hear the words, but he can see Father John's face: the way he nods, the way his expression shifts, the way he glances toward the door where Lem is standing.

Their eyes meet. Lem and Father John. Across the length of the nave, through the double doors.

Something passes between them. The same thing that passed at the communion rail. Recognition. Fear. The shared knowledge of something that shouldn't be possible but is.

Father John looks away first.

He says something to Beth. She nods. Touches his arm briefly. Then she turns and walks back toward Lem.

"What did you tell him?" Lem asks when she reaches him.

"I asked if we could meet with him this week." Her voice is steady, but her eyes are bright with unshed tears. "I told him something's happening to you. That I'm worried. That I need help."

Lem nods slowly. He should feel betrayed. Should feel exposed. But he doesn't. He's too tired. Too emptied out. Too full of everything that happened in that sanctuary.

"What did he say?"

"He said yes. Wednesday." She pauses. Looks at him. "He said he's worried too. He said he saw something today. During the service. He said he doesn't know what it was, but he saw it."

Lem closes his eyes.

He saw it.

Of course he did. He felt it at the communion rail. The presence that filled the space between them. The light that spilled out of whatever is happening to Lem.

Father John saw it. And now he's scared too. Everyone is scared except Lem.

Because Lem isn't scared anymore. He's terrified and he's certain and he's broken and he's whole. He's all of those things at once, and he doesn't know how to explain it to anyone, not even himself.

He opens his eyes. Takes Beth's hand.

"Let's go home," he says.

They walk to the car. The sky is hard and blue. The bells are ringing. The world goes on.

And somewhere inside Lem, three dreams burn like coals, waiting for the moment when he'll finally have to speak.

Chapter Seven

Kate

S he arrives a little after two.

Lem hears the car before he sees it: the crunch of gravel in the driveway, the engine cutting off, the door closing. He's standing at the kitchen window, the same window where he's stood every morning since this began, looking out at the water without seeing it.

Beth is already moving. He hears her footsteps in the hall, the front door opening, and then the sounds he knows so well, mother and daughter, the particular music of their greeting. Beth's voice rises with something like relief, then drops into the low murmur of concern. He can't make out the words, but he knows what they're saying. He knows Beth is telling her everything: the sleeplessness, the silence, the weeping in church. The husband who won't speak. The father who has gone somewhere she can't follow.

He should go to them. Should greet his daughter, hold her, tell her everything is fine.

But everything is not fine. And he's tired of pretending.

He stays at the window. Watches the heron in the shallows. Waits.

* * *

Beth holds Kate longer than usual, she always does now. Every visit, every embrace, carries the weight of expectation. Kate is 29, unmarried,

married to her career instead. Doctor at Duke Medical School, youngest in her department, published in journals Lem can't pronounce. He is proud of her, fiercely, uncomplicated proud. But Beth wants more. Beth wants a ring, a name, a nursery to decorate. She wants grandchildren while she is still young enough to chase them.

Kate bears it with patience. She always has. Even as a teenager, she'd never fought the way other kids fought, she just watched, waited, made her own choices in her own time. And Beth has learned to hold her questions, mostly, letting them live in the length of her embraces instead of in words.

Today, though, the questions don't come. Today there is only fear.

"He's in the kitchen," Beth says quietly. "He won't talk to me. He hasn't really talked to me in days."

Kate nods. Squeezes her mother's hands. Turns toward the house.

* * *

Footsteps behind him. Lighter than Beth's. He knows the sound of her walk, has known it since she was a toddler, those first unsteady steps across this same kitchen floor.

"Dad."

He turns.

Kate is standing in the doorway. Twenty-nine years old, her mother's eyes, her father's stubborn jaw. She's dressed simply: jeans, her hair pulled back, a Duke sweatshirt, because she never missed a chance to needle him. No makeup. She left in a hurry; he can see that. Dropped whatever she was doing and drove three hours because her mother called.

Because of him.

He looks at her, and for a moment he doesn't see the woman. He sees the infant, six weeks old, wrapped in white, held in his arms at the font of St. Paul's. His father's hands, weathered and steady, pouring the water. His father's voice, speaking not to Kate but to him:

"Will you be responsible for the Christian upbringing of this child?"

He had answered without hesitation. *I will, with God's help.* And he had meant it, meant it with everything he was. Every Sunday in that pew. Every Christmas Eve when they walked into St. Paul's together. Kate in her acolyte robes, carrying the cross down the aisle. Kate in the choir loft, her voice rising with the hymns. Eighteen years of formation, of showing up, of building faith into her bones the only way he knew how, through presence, through repetition, through the steady rhythm of a life lived in the pews.

His father had watched him choose Chapel Hill over the Citadel, the liberal bastion of the South instead of military tradition. There had been chagrin, disappointment that lived in silences rather than arguments. But his father had also given him the book, had written the inscription that Lem still carried: *I believe you will write your own one day.*

And he had baptized Kate. That was the last sacred act between them: grandfather, son, granddaughter. The water. The vow. The chain unbroken.

Now Kate was a doctor, a professor, still Episcopalian, she went when she could, not every Sunday anymore, but she hadn't left the church. She'd followed his footsteps to Carolina for undergrad, to his delight. Then chosen Duke for medical school, to his theatrical grief. "Tar Heel born, Tar Heel bred," he used to say when she was a girl. "Tar Heel undergrad," she'd shoot back now, "Duke-trained physician." It was their old argument, worn comfortable as a favorite jacket.

He had kept the vow. Whatever else was happening to him now, he had kept it.

"Hey, Katie."

She crosses the kitchen and wraps her arms around him. He holds her, this grown woman who will always be his little girl, who used to fall asleep on his chest, who learned to cast a lure before she learned to ride a bike.

She doesn't say anything. Just holds on.

After a long moment, she pulls back. Looks at him. Studies his face the way she always has, direct, unflinching, seeing more than he wants her to see. But there's something else now, something he recognizes. The physician's gaze. She is assessing him. Clinically. Running through possibilities, ruling them out one by one. Orientation, coherence, affect. The daughter in her listening; the doctor in her taking notes.

"You look terrible," she says.

He almost smiles. "Thanks."

"I mean it. When's the last time you slept?"

"I don't know. A while."

She nods slowly. Doesn't push. That's Kate. She's never pushed. She gathers information. Makes her own judgments in her own time.

"Mom's worried," she says.

"I know."

"She said you won't talk to her. Said something happened at church this morning."

He looks away.

"Something's been happening," he says quietly. "I don't know how to explain it."

"Try."

He shakes his head. "Not here. Not in the kitchen."

She's quiet for a moment. Then she moves to stand beside him at the window, looking out at the water. The dock. The boat.

"Take me out, Dad."

He glances at her.

"A boat ride," she says. "Like we used to do."

The words hit him somewhere deep. *Like we used to do.* Saturday afternoons when she was a girl, just the two of them on the water, no destination, no purpose. Drifting through the marsh while he taught her the names of things: the birds, the fish, the grasses. The way the light changed over the sound. How to read the water by its color. The way the world went quiet when you got far enough from shore.

She's asking him to go back there. To the place where words come easier.

"Okay," he says. "Okay."

* * *

Beth is on the porch when they come out.

She's sitting in the rocker, her hands wrapped around a mug of tea that's probably gone cold. She watches them walk across the yard, father and daughter, side by side, and Lem can see the fear in her face. The hope, too. The desperate wish that Kate can reach him in ways she can't.

"We're going out for a bit," Kate says.

Beth nods. Doesn't argue. "How long?"

"I don't know. A while."

Beth looks at Kate, and Lem sees it, the question that lives beneath every question. *You drove three hours. You dropped everything. Are you eating? Are you sleeping? Is there anyone?* The words she can't stop herself from asking, even now, even when everything else is falling apart. She wants Kate settled. Wants her happy in the way Beth understands happiness: a husband, a home, children underfoot. Kate has chosen differently, and Beth has never stopped grieving it, even as she's learned to hold her tongue.

"Be careful," Beth says. To both of them, but her eyes are on Lem.

He stops at the bottom of the porch steps. Looks up at his wife.

"I'm sorry," he says. "For all of this. I'm sorry."

Her eyes glisten. She presses her lips together, holding something back.

"Just come home," she says. "Whatever's happening, just come home."

He nods. Turns. Walks with Kate toward the dock.

He can feel Beth's gaze on his back the whole way. He doesn't turn around.

* * *

The Pathfinder rocks gently as they step aboard.

Lem goes through the motions without thinking: checking the fuel, starting the engine, letting it idle while Kate unties the lines. She moves easily on the boat, comfortable, sure-footed. He taught her this. Taught her everything she knows about the water.

She coils the bow line and takes her place on the bench seat behind the console. The same seat where the stranger sat, that first morning. Lem pushes the thought away. Not yet.

He eases the throttle forward. The boat pulls away from the dock, the house shrinking behind them, the shore falling away.

The afternoon is bright and cool, the sky a hard December blue. The water is calm, barely a ripple, the marsh grass standing still in the windless air. A pair of pelicans glide low over the surface, their wings nearly touching the water.

Lem steers toward the open sound, keeping the speed low. The engine hums. The wake spreads out behind them in a gentle V.

Kate doesn't speak. She's waiting. Giving him space.

They pass near the oyster bars where he caught the redfish. Was that only two days ago? It feels like weeks. Months. The days have lost their shape, blurred together by the dreams and the sleeplessness and the weight of everything he can't say.

He cuts the engine.

The boat drifts. The silence settles over them, not the tense silence of the house, but something softer. The lap of water against the hull. The distant cry of a gull. The small sounds of the world going on.

Kate shifts on the bench. Draws her knees up. Waits.

Lem stands at the console, hands resting on the wheel, looking out at the water. The marsh stretches away on both sides, green and gold in the afternoon light. A heron lifts off from the shallows, its wings beating slow and heavy, and disappears into the distance.

"I've been dreaming," he says.

His voice sounds strange to him. Rusty. Like a door that hasn't been opened in years.

Kate doesn't respond. Just listens.

"Not regular dreams. Something else."

He pauses. Tries to find the words. They've been locked inside him for days, pressing against his ribs, demanding release. Now that he's finally speaking, they come slowly. Reluctantly. As if they're not sure they want to be spoken.

"It started last week. Wednesday night, I think. I was on the boat, this boat, but it wasn't... it wasn't a normal dream. The colors were wrong. Too bright. Too real. The water was like glass."

He stops. Swallows.

"There was a man. Sitting right where you're sitting now. I didn't see him at first. I was fishing, casting toward the marsh, and nothing was biting. And then he spoke. He said, 'Try the other side.'"

Kate is very still. Watching him.

"I argued with him. Told him the fish were in the shallows, not the deep water. I've been fishing this sound my whole life. I know where the fish are. But he just kept saying it. 'Try the other side.' So finally I did."

He shakes his head slowly. The memory is so vivid, so present. He can feel the rod in his hands, the tug of the line, the weight of the fish.

"I caught one immediately. First cast. And I brought it in, and I knelt down to release it, and I said what I always say, 'Thank you, God.' And then he was beside me. Kneeling next to me at the rail. And he said..."

His voice breaks. He has to stop. Breathe.

"He said, 'The kingdom of the Father is spread out upon the earth, and people do not see it.'"

The words hang in the air between them. The boat rocks gently. The water laps at the hull.

"And then I looked at him. At his face. And I knew. I knew who he was. I can't explain exactly how, but I knew. And I reached for him, and I woke up."

He turns to look at Kate. She's still watching him, her face unreadable. Not skeptical. Not afraid. Just... listening. But he can see it working behind her eyes, the physician's mind, sorting, categorizing, running differentials. *Neurological event. Sleep disorder. Temporal lobe activity. Early onset dementia.* She can't help it. It is how she's been trained.

"My pillow was soaked. I'd been crying in my sleep. And the dream didn't fade. That's what was strange. Usually dreams dissolve when you wake up. But this one stayed. It's still there. I can see it right now, as clearly as I can see you."

Kate is quiet for a long moment. Then she asks, softly, "Who was he, Dad?"

Lem closes his eyes.

"You know who he was."

She doesn't respond.

"The second dream was different," he continues. "I was on Shackleford. The sound side, where we used to anchor and play on the beach when you were little. There was a child, a boy, maybe eight or nine, sitting in the shallows, building a sandcastle in the sand. And I walked toward him, and he looked up at me, and he started asking me questions."

He opens his eyes. Looks out at the water.

"He asked me when my work became work. When I stopped doing things for the joy of it. He said I'd made two things out of what was supposed to be one."

He pauses. The words are harder now. Closer to the bone.

"He said, 'Why do you hold so tightly to what washes away?' And I looked at his hands, he was still building, still shaping the sand, and I saw the scars. In his palms. Old scars. Healed."

Kate draws a sharp breath. Lem doesn't look at her.

"I reached for him. And I woke up."

The boat drifts. A cormorant surfaces nearby, shakes the water from its wings, and dives again.

"And the third one?" Kate asks quietly.

Lem nods. He knew she would ask. She's always been thorough.

"Last night. I was at the fish house, the old one, where Captain Roy used to sell his catch. There was a man sitting on the dock, mending a net. He looked like Captain Roy, but it wasn't him. He invited me to sit. Gave me a net needle. We worked together for a long time without talking."

He can feel it now: the weight of the net needle in his hand, the rhythm of the work, the silence that wasn't empty but full.

"He said I'd been looking for him in the wrong places. High places. Churches and books and ideas. He said, 'But I'm here.' And then he said..."

His voice catches again. The words are so heavy. So true.

"'Split a piece of driftwood. I am there. Lift a shell, and you will find me.'"

Kate is crying. He can hear it in her breathing, the slight hitch, the careful control. She's trying not to let him see.

"And then I asked him. The question I've been asking since the first dream. I said, 'Why are you speaking to me?' And he said..."

Lem turns to face her. His daughter. His Katie. Tears streaming down her face now, not hiding anymore.

"He said, 'Because you've been speaking to me your whole life. You just didn't know I was listening.'"

The words fall between them like an anchor finding bottom.

Kate wipes her face with the back of her hand. Sniffs. Looks at him with those eyes, her mother's eyes, but something else in them now. Something he hasn't seen before.

"Dad," she says. "Do you know what you're telling me?"

"Yes."

"You're saying..."

"I know what I'm saying."

She shakes her head. Not in denial. In wonder. But also in struggle, he can see it, the war inside her. The daughter who knew him, who trusted him, who had never known him to lie or exaggerate or imagine things. And the physician who had been trained to see pathology, to diagnose, to find the medical explanation that made the impossible make sense.

"How do you know? How can you be sure it's not just... dreams? Stress? Your mind playing tricks?"

He considers the question. He's asked it himself, a hundred times, lying awake in the dark, wondering if he's losing his mind.

"I can't prove it," he says. "I can't give you evidence. All I can tell you is what I know. And I know. I *know*, Katie, that these dreams are not ordinary dreams. I know that I'm being visited. I know that the one visiting me is..."

He can't say the name. Not yet. It's too big. Too holy.

"I know who he is," he finishes quietly. "And I know he's real."

Kate is silent for a long time. The boat drifts. The sun is lower now, the light turning gold, the shadows lengthening across the water.

Finally, she speaks.

"I've seen psychosis, Dad." Her voice is measured, careful, the voice she uses with patients, he imagines. "I've seen delusion. I've seen what a brain tumor can do, what temporal lobe seizures look like, what early-onset dementia presents as." She pauses. "This isn't that. You're oriented. You're coherent. You're not exhibiting any of the markers I'd expect if this were..."

She stops. Shakes her head.

"I don't know what this is. But I know what it isn't."

Lem feels something loosen in his chest.

"I still go, Dad." Her voice is softer now. "To church. Not every Sunday, not like you and Mom. My schedule doesn't allow it. But I haven't left. I'm still there. Still part of it." She looks out at the water. "I carried that cross down the aisle for six years. I sang in that choir. I know the liturgy in my bones, you made sure of that. You and Mom. Every Sunday, no exceptions."

She turns back to him.

"What you're describing... it doesn't fit anything I was taught. It doesn't fit the theology, the tradition, any of it. But I know you. And you're the most grounded person I've ever met. You don't make things up. You don't imagine things. You never have."

She holds his gaze.

"I believe *you*."

Lem's eyes blur. The tears he's been fighting all day, all week, break through again. He doesn't try to stop them. He lets them fall, standing there at the console of his boat, his daughter watching him cry.

"I'm scared, Katie. I'm scared of what's happening. I'm scared of what it means. I'm scared that I'm going to lose everything: your mother, my work, my life. And I'm scared that even if I don't lose any of that, I'll never be the same. I can't go back to who I was before this started. I don't know how."

Kate stands. Crosses the deck. Wraps her arms around him the way she did in the kitchen, but different now. Not comfort for a parent who seems unwell. Something else.

Witness.

She's witnessing him. Holding what he's given her. Not explaining it. Not fixing it. Not running differentials or recommending specialists. Just *being there*, the way he was there for her when she was small and the world was too big and too frightening.

"You don't have to go back," she says into his shoulder. "You just have to go forward. And you don't have to do it alone."

He holds his daughter. The boat rocks beneath them. The water shimmers in the golden light.

And for the first time since the dreams began, Lem feels something like peace.

Not understanding. Not resolution. Just the simple, profound relief of being known.

* * *

They stay out until the sun touches the marsh.

They don't talk much more, there's nothing more to say, not yet. Kate asks a few questions, small ones. What did his face look like? What did his voice sound like? Lem answers as best he can, though the answers feel inadequate. How do you describe a face that changes every time you see it but is always the same? How do you capture a voice that sounds like every voice you've ever loved? And the eyes, how can he describe the eyes?

Eventually, he starts the engine. Turns the boat toward home. The dock appears ahead, the house rising behind it, the windows glowing in the fading light.

Beth is still on the porch. Waiting.

Lem ties up the boat. Kate climbs onto the dock first, then turns to offer him her hand. He takes it. Steps onto the weathered boards.

They walk toward the house together. Father and daughter. Something sealed between them now, something that will hold.

Beth stands as they approach. Her face is tight with questions, with fear, with the desperate need to know what happened out there.

Kate reaches her first. Puts her arms around her mother. Holds her.

"He's okay, Mom," she says quietly. "He's not crazy. Something's happening to him, and I don't understand it, but he's okay."

Beth looks over Kate's shoulder at Lem. Searching his face.

He nods. It's all he can offer.

She closes her eyes. Lets out a breath she seems to have been holding for days.

"Come inside," she says. "Both of you. I'll make dinner."

They walk into the house together. The door closes behind them.

Outside, the heron returns to the shallows. The last light fades from the water. The stars begin to appear, one by one, in the darkening sky.

And somewhere out there, beyond the marsh, beyond the sound, beyond the edge of sleep, the dreams are waiting.

Chapter Eight

Still Waters

He sleeps.

That's the miracle of Sunday night: he sleeps. No dreams. No visitors. No waking in the dark with his arm outstretched and his face wet with tears. Just sleep, deep and dark and dreamless, the kind of sleep he hasn't had in what feels like years.

He wakes Monday morning to gray light and the sound of rain.

For a long moment he just lies there, listening. The soft patter on the roof. The drip from the gutter he keeps meaning to fix. Beth breathing beside him, still asleep, her hand curled on the pillow near her face.

He feels... quiet. That's the only word for it. The churning inside him has stilled. The dreams are there, he can feel them, stored somewhere deep, but they're not pressing against him the way they were. They're resting too.

He gets up slowly, careful not to wake Beth, and goes downstairs.

Kate is in the kitchen.

She's standing at the window with a mug of coffee, watching the rain fall on the water. She turns when she hears him, and something in her face shifts, not worry, not anymore. Something softer. Something like wonder.

"You slept," she says.

"I did."

"You look better."

He pours himself a cup of coffee. Stands beside her at the window. The bay is silver-gray, the rain dimpling the surface, the marsh fading into mist.

"I feel better," he says. And it's true. Not fixed. Not resolved. But better. Lighter. As if something that was clenched inside him has finally let go.

They stand there together, father and daughter, watching the rain. Not talking. Not needing to.

After a while, Kate says, "I should head back this afternoon. Work tomorrow."

He nods. He knew she couldn't stay forever. But he's grateful, more grateful than he knows how to say. For the moment. For her presence. For the way she listened without judging, believed without understanding.

"Thank you," he says. "For coming. For... all of it."

She looks at him. Those eyes, her mother's eyes, holding something new now. A kind of respect that goes deeper than the usual father-daughter bond.

"Call me," she says. "After you see Father John. Tell me what happens."

"I will."

She reaches over and squeezes his arm. Then she turns back to the window, and they watch the rain together until Beth comes downstairs.

* * *

He doesn't write.

The thought occurs to him, sometime mid-morning, the laptop in his office, the empty document, the deadline that hasn't gone away. But the thought doesn't carry the weight it used to. It's just a fact, sitting alongside other facts. The rain on the roof. The coffee in his cup. The work that will or won't come.

Instead, he finds himself in the garage, looking at the toolbox he hasn't opened in months.

The house needs things. It always needs things, that's the nature of a house near the water, where the salt air eats at everything, where the moisture works its way into wood and metal and bone. He's been ignoring the list for too long, lost in the book that won't come, the dreams that wouldn't stop.

But today the list feels different. Not burden. Just work. Simple, honest work.

He starts with the porch. The third board from the steps has been loose since summer, creaking every time someone walks across it. He kneels down, pulls the old nails, fits the board back into place. The hammer feels good in his hand. The nails sink into the wood with a satisfying thunk.

Split a piece of driftwood. I am there.

The words rise in him, unbidden, but they don't startle him. They feel true. The hammer. The nail. The wood. All of it holy, if you know how to look.

He moves on to the gutter. Gets the ladder from the garage, climbs up, clears out the leaves and debris that have been collecting since fall. The rain has stopped, but the world is still wet, still gray, still quiet. From up here he can see the whole property: the house, the dock, the boat, the marsh stretching away toward the sound.

It's beautiful. It's always been beautiful. But today he sees it differently. Today it looks like what it is. A gift. A life. A kingdom spread out before him, waiting to be noticed.

He climbs down. Finds more work. The dripping faucet in the kitchen. The cabinet door that won't close right. Small things. Simple things. The work of hands.

* * *

Kate leaves in the early afternoon.

She hugs Beth first, a long embrace, the two of them holding each other in the driveway, words passing between them that Lem can't hear. Then she comes to him.

"You seem better, Dad," she says.

"I think I am."

"Whatever's happening to you..." She pauses. Shakes her head. "I don't understand it. But I believe it's real. And I believe you're going to be okay."

He pulls her close. Holds her the way he used to hold her when she was small. She's taller than Beth now, almost as tall as him, but in his arms she's still his little girl. Still the one he taught to cast a lure, to read the water, to say thank you for every fish.

"I love you, Katie."

"I love you too, Dad."

She pulls back. Wipes her eyes. Gets in her car.

He and Beth stand in the driveway, watching until the car disappears around the bend. Then Beth reaches over and takes his hand.

"She's a good girl," Beth says.

"She is."

They walk back inside together.

* * *

That night, dinner is quiet.

Beth makes soup, something simple, warming, the kind of meal that asks nothing of you. They eat at the kitchen table, the window dark, the sound of the water invisible but present.

They don't talk about the dreams. They don't talk about Father John. They talk about the porch board, the gutter, the faucet that finally stopped dripping. They talk about Kate's drive home, whether she'll hit traffic, whether she'll remember to eat the leftovers Beth packed for her.

Ordinary things. The small currency of a long marriage.

After dinner, Lem washes the dishes while Beth dries. They've done this thousands of times, the ritual of it, the rhythm. His hands in the warm water. Her hands with the towel. The clink of plates, the soft conversation, the life they've built together.

He looks at her. Really looks. The gray in her hair that wasn't there when they married. The lines around her eyes. The way she moves, efficient and graceful, the same way she's always moved.

"I love you," he says.

She stops. Looks at him. Something flickers in her eyes, surprise, maybe, or relief.

"I love you too," she says.

He dries his hands. Takes the towel from her. Pulls her into his arms.

They stand there in the kitchen, holding each other, not speaking. The house settles around them. The water laps at the dock. The world goes on.

* * *

He sleeps again Monday night.

No dreams. Just rest.

Tuesday morning, he wakes before dawn.

The house is dark, Beth still sleeping. He lies there for a moment, feeling the stillness, then gets up and goes to the window.

The sky is just beginning to lighten, a thin line of gray on the horizon, the stars fading, the water black and smooth. The Pathfinder is a dark shape at the end of the dock, rocking gently.

He knows, without deciding, that he's going out today.

He dresses quietly. Makes coffee. Lets Duke out, then back in. The dog looks at him with knowing eyes, tail already wagging.

"Yeah," Lem says. "You can come."

* * *

The water is glass.

He idles out from the dock as the light grows, the engine barely above a whisper, Duke standing in the bow with his nose lifted to the wind. The marsh slides past on either side, the marsh grass catching the first gold of sunrise, the birds beginning to stir.

He doesn't have a destination. Doesn't have a plan. He just lets the boat carry him, following the channels he's followed his whole life, reading the water the way Captain Roy taught him.

The sun clears the horizon. The light spills across the sound, turning everything gold and rose and burning. Lem cuts the engine and lets the boat drift.

He picks up a rod. Not because he needs to catch anything, the freezer is still full, Beth was right about that, but because it's what his hands know how to do. He ties on a lure, something simple, and casts toward the marsh edge.

The line arcs out over the water. The lure lands with a soft splash. He works it back slowly, feeling the weight of it, the resistance of the water.

Nothing bites. He doesn't care.

He casts again. And again. The rhythm of it, the cast, the retrieve, the cast, emptying his mind, filling his body. Duke settles in the bow, chin on paws, watching the birds.

The morning passes. The sun climbs. The water shimmers.

He catches a few fish, small ones, nothing to keep. Each time, he brings them to the side of the boat, holds them for a moment in the water, feels their heartbeat against his palm.

"Thank you, God," he murmurs. The same words he's always said. But they mean something different now.

He releases each fish and watches it disappear into the dark water.

* * *

He comes home in the late afternoon.

Beth is on the porch, a book open in her lap, though he can tell she hasn't been reading. She's been watching the water. Waiting for him.

He ties up the boat. Walks up the dock. Duke trots ahead, already looking for his dinner.

"Catch anything?" Beth asks.

"A few. Let them go."

She nods. Studies his face. He doesn't know what she sees there, but whatever it is, it seems to ease something in her.

"Good day?" she asks.

"Yeah." He sits down in the chair beside her. "Good day."

They watch the light change over the water. The gold deepening to amber. The shadows lengthening across the marsh. A heron glides in and lands in the shallows, settling into its eternal stillness.

"Tomorrow," Beth says quietly.

"I know."

"Are you ready?"

He considers the question. Is he ready to sit in Father John's office and try to explain what's been happening? Is he ready to watch the priest's face as he describes the dreams, the visitors, the words that won't let him go?

"I don't know," he says honestly. "But I'll go."

She reaches over. Takes his hand. Holds it.

They sit together as the sun sinks toward the marsh, as the first stars begin to appear, as the world goes quiet around them.

* * *

That night, they go to bed early.

Beth falls asleep quickly, her breathing slow and even. Lem lies beside her, looking at the ceiling, waiting for the familiar dread to rise, the fear of what the night might bring, what dreams might come.

But the dread doesn't come. Just peace. Just stillness.

He closes his eyes.

The kingdom of the Father is spread out upon the earth, and people do not see it.

But he sees it now. In the light on the water. In the work of his hands. In his daughter's face. In his wife's touch.

He sees it.

He sleeps.

Chapter Nine

Tuesday Night

The cold hits him first.

A December night on the waterfront, the kind of cold that comes off the water and settles into your bones. He's standing on the dock, the main dock, the one that runs past the bait shop and the fuel pump and the slips where the charter boats tie up.

He knows this place. Has walked it a thousand times.

But now it's night, and the dock is empty, and the only light comes from a single lamp at the far end, casting a yellow circle on the weathered boards. Beyond it, further down the waterfront, the windows of Mike's glow faintly, the old restaurant, the one Captain Roy used to take him to during those summer weeks, the one he hasn't visited in years.

He doesn't know how he got here.

The boards are wet beneath his feet. It's been raining, he can smell it in the air, can see the puddles gathered in the low spots, the dark stains where water has soaked into the wood. The whole dock glistens under the lamp.

A man is sitting on a bench near the lamp.

Lem has passed this bench countless times. An old bench, paint peeling, bolted to the dock decades ago. He's never given it a second thought. Just another piece of the waterfront, as invisible as the pilings and the cleats and the coiled lines.

A man is sitting there now.

And the bench is dry.

Lem stops. Stares. The rain has touched everything: the boards, the pilings, the coiled lines, his own clothes already damp from the mist. But the bench where the man sits is bone dry. As if the water parted around it. As if the rain refused to fall there.

A dog lies curled at the man's feet. A stray, thin, ribs showing, the kind of dog that lives on scraps and luck. It should be watching the man, hoping for food, the way strays do.

But the dog is watching Lem.

Its eyes follow him as he approaches, steady and unblinking, as if Lem is the one who needs watching. As if Lem is the one who might run.

Lem walks toward them. His footsteps make no sound. The water laps at the pilings. The boats creak in their slips.

As he gets closer, he sees the man more clearly. Old coat, frayed at the cuffs. Knit cap pulled low. Hands folded in his lap, still and patient. A face weathered by years of wind and sun and cold, or maybe by something else. Something harder than weather.

Lem has seen this man before.

The realization hits him like a physical blow. He has *seen* him, right here, on this dock, on this bench. Walked past him on the way to his boat. Walked past without stopping. Without speaking. Without *seeing*.

The man doesn't look up as Lem approaches. Just sits there, hands folded, eyes fixed on the dark water.

Lem stops a few feet away. He doesn't know what to say.

Finally, the man speaks.

"You can sit, if you want."

The voice is quiet. Rough. The voice of someone who doesn't use it much.

Lem sits. The bench is dry beneath him, impossibly dry in all this wet. The lamp hums overhead. The water moves in the darkness beyond the dock.

They sit together in silence. The dog's eyes never leave Lem's face.

Lem tries to remember how many times he's passed this bench. How many times this man, or someone like him, was sitting here. How many times he looked the other way, walked a little faster, pretended not to see.

"I've seen you before," he says finally. "Haven't I?"

"You've seen me." The man nods slowly. Still not looking at him.

"I didn't stop," says Lem.

"No."

The word hangs in the air. No accusation in it. Just fact.

"I didn't..." Lem's voice catches. "I don't know why I didn't stop."

The man is quiet for a long moment. Then he says:

"You were busy. You had somewhere to be. I understand. Everyone has somewhere to be."

But the words don't feel like absolution. They feel like a mirror.

"You said something once," the man continues, his voice low. "Years ago. You were walking to your boat, early morning, and you passed a man sleeping under the awning of the bait shop. And you said, under your breath, not meaning for anyone to hear, you said, 'There but for the grace of God.'"

Lem's blood goes cold.

He remembers that morning. Ten years ago, maybe more. He remembers the man under the awning, the mutter under his breath, the way he kept walking without stopping.

He never told anyone about that moment. Never spoke those words aloud again.

"How do you know that?" he whispers.

The man doesn't answer. Just lets the question hang.

"Yesterday," the man says. "You walked past. The day before that, too. I was hungry. I was thirsty. I was a stranger."

Lem's chest tightens. The words are familiar, he's heard them in church, read them in Scripture. But hearing them here, on this dock, from this man's lips, they sound different. They sound like confession. Like indictment.

"I didn't know," Lem whispers.

"Didn't you?"

The question isn't harsh. It's almost gentle. Which makes it worse.

"You knew," the man continues. "Everyone knows. They just don't want to see. It's easier to walk past. To look the other way. To tell yourself it's not your problem."

He turns, finally, and looks at Lem.

The face is weathered. Lined. Ordinary. The face of a man who has lived on the margins, who has been overlooked and forgotten, who has become invisible to the world that walks past him every day.

"Love your brother as your own soul," the man says. "Protect him as you would the pupil of your eye."

He pauses. His eyes, dark, deep, hold Lem's.

"But you didn't see me. How can you protect what you don't see? How can you love what you refuse to look at?"

Lem is weeping. He doesn't try to stop it.

"I'm sorry," he says. "I'm so sorry."

The man reaches over. His hand, rough, weathered, cold, rests on Lem's arm.

"You've been a passerby your whole life," he says. "Walking past. Not stopping. There's no shame in it. That's what the world teaches. Keep moving. Don't get involved. Protect yourself."

His grip tightens. Just slightly.

"But I'm asking you to stop now. To see. To sit with what you've been walking past."

Lem looks at him. The tears are cooling on his cheeks in the cold night air.

"Whatever you did for the least of these," the man says, "you did for me."

He pauses.

"Whatever you *didn't* do..."

He doesn't finish the sentence. He doesn't have to.

The man releases Lem's arm. Folds his hands back in his lap. Returns his gaze to the dark water.

The dog at his feet finally looks away from Lem. Lowers its head. Closes its eyes.

"There's a light on in the diner," the man says quietly. "Down the way. Looks warm in there."

Lem turns. Looks toward Mike's. The windows glow yellow against the night, fogged with warmth, a beacon at the edge of the cold dock.

"You should go," the man says. "Someone's waiting for you."

Lem looks back at him. Wants to say something: what, he doesn't know. Thank you. Forgive me. Don't let me forget.

But the man is staring at the water again, still and patient, as if Lem has already gone.

Lem stands. His legs are unsteady. The cold has seeped into him, or maybe it's something else, the weight of what he's just heard, the shame of what he's just seen in himself.

He walks toward the light.

* * *

He's sitting in a booth by the window.

He doesn't remember entering. Doesn't remember opening the door, crossing inside, sliding onto the cracked vinyl seat. But here he is, Mike's, the old waterfront restaurant, the smell of coffee and fried fish thick in the air.

A coffee cup sits in front of him, half empty, gone cold. The restaurant is nearly deserted, just one other figure at the far end of the counter, hunched over a plate. The fluorescent lights hum.

The clock on the wall reads 3:47.

Lem stares at it. 3:47. The hands aren't moving. He watches for a long moment, waiting for the minute to change, but it doesn't. The clock is frozen.

3:47 a.m.

The time he was born. His mother told him once, years ago: *You came into the world at 3:47 in the morning. I remember because the nurse said it was the hour when the veil between worlds was thinnest.*

He'd forgotten that. Hadn't thought of it in decades.

But the clock remembers.

Through the fogged window, he can see the dock. The bench. But the man is gone. Or maybe he was never there. Or maybe he's always there, and Lem just never stopped to see.

He wraps his hands around the cold coffee cup. His fingers are trembling.

Footsteps behind him. The soft sound of someone approaching.

"Warm that up for you?"

He turns.

She's standing beside the booth, coffee pot in hand. A woman in her fifties, maybe older, hard to tell. The kind of face that's been weathered by work and time, the lines around her eyes speaking of early mornings and late nights and not enough rest in between. Her uniform is faded, her name tag says *Darlene*, and there's something in the way she holds herself, patient, unhurried, like she's got nowhere else to be.

"Sure," he says. His voice is hoarse. "Thanks."

She pours. And pours. And pours.

Lem watches the coffee rise in his cup, past half full, past three-quarters, nearly to the rim. But she keeps pouring, and the pot keeps giving, and he realizes with a start that the pot should be empty by now. She's poured enough to fill three cups. Four. The stream of coffee keeps coming, dark and hot and endless.

She stops. Sets the pot on the table. The pot looks exactly as full as when she started.

Lem stares at it. Says nothing.

She doesn't seem to notice. She slides into the booth across from him, and before she sits, she places something on the table. A plate. A slice of pie, apple, with a lattice crust, a scoop of vanilla ice cream already melting on top.

"I didn't order that," he says.

"No," she agrees. "But it's what you wanted."

He looks at the pie. His throat tightens.

Apple pie with ice cream. His grandmother used to make it, when he was a boy. Saturday nights at her house, after dinner, the smell of cinnamon filling the kitchen. He hasn't eaten it since she died. Hasn't even thought about it.

But he wanted it. Somewhere deep, in a place he doesn't have words for, he wanted it.

"You've been sitting here a while," she says. Not an accusation. Just an observation.

"I guess I have."

She looks at him with eyes that see too much.

"You look like you've seen a ghost."

He almost laughs. Almost.

"Something like that."

"You want to tell me about it?"

He opens his mouth. Closes it. What is there to tell? The man on the bench? The dreams that won't stop? The face that appears at the moment of waking, always dissolving before he can hold it?

"I don't know where to start," he says.

"That's usually where it starts," she says. "Not knowing."

He stares at the coffee. The steam rising. The dark surface reflecting the fluorescent lights.

"I've been carrying something," he says finally. "For a while now. And I don't know what to do with it."

She nods. Waits.

"People are worried about me. My wife. My daughter. They think something's wrong."

"Is something wrong?"

He looks up at her. Her face is calm, open, without judgment.

"I don't know," he says. "Something's *happening*. But I don't know if it's wrong. I don't know if it's right. I just know it won't stop."

"And you haven't told anyone what it is."

It's not a question. He looks at her sharply.

"I've told some people. Pieces of it. But the real thing, what's really happening, who's really..."

He trails off. She's watching him with a patience that feels infinite.

"Why not?" she asks.

"Because they'll think I'm crazy. Because I'm not sure I'm not crazy. Because..."

"Because you're afraid."

The words land in him like stones.

"Yes," he whispers. "I'm afraid."

She reaches across the table. Her hand covers his, rough, warm, the hand of someone who has worked every day of her life.

"You're carrying something," she says. "I can see it. It's pressing on you from the inside. Pressing to get out."

He can't speak. His throat is tight.

"There's nothing hidden that won't be revealed," she says. "What's in front of your face, you need to recognize. What's hidden from you will become plain. But first..."

She leans closer. Her eyes are dark, deep, filled with something he can't name.

"You have to bring forth what's inside you. It's the only thing that saves."

He shakes his head. "I don't know how."

"Yes, you do. You're a writer. You know how to put words on a page. You've just been afraid to write *these* words."

"But why..." His voice breaks. "Why does it come like this? In dreams? In... in forms I almost recognize? Why not just..."

"Just plainly?" She almost smiles. Something sad in it. "Truth doesn't come into the world naked. It never has. It comes in types and images. In forms you can receive. That's not deception. That's mercy."

She squeezes his hand.

"You couldn't bear the full light. Not yet. So it comes to you gently. In disguises. In faces you can look at without being destroyed."

He's crying now. He doesn't know when he started. The tears fall onto the table, onto their joined hands, and she doesn't pull away.

"What you carry inside," she says, her voice low and certain, "bring it out. Bring it forth. If you do, it will save you."

She pauses. Her grip tightens on his hand.

"If you don't, if you keep it locked inside, if you refuse to speak, it will destroy you. Not because it wants to. Because that's what happens to truth that's denied its voice."

He looks at her. Really looks. The lined face. The tired eyes. The ordinary uniform with the name tag that says *Darlene.*

"Who are you?" he whispers.

She doesn't answer. Just holds his gaze.

And then the face shifts.

Just for an instant. The features rearranging into something else, something ancient and familiar, something he has seen on a boat at dawn, on a shore, on a dock behind the fish house, on a bench in the cold.

The eyes.

Always the eyes.

He reaches for her...

And wakes in the dark, his hand extended, grasping at nothing.

* * *

The bedroom is gray with early light.

Lem lies on his back, staring at the ceiling, his body trembling, his face wet with tears.

But his hand, the hand she held, is warm. Unnaturally warm. As if her grip is still there, her rough palm still pressed against his skin. He brings it to his chest and feels the heat radiating from it, a warmth that shouldn't exist, that has no source, that lingers like a blessing.

One dream. Two encounters.

I was hungry. I was thirsty. I was a stranger.

Bring forth what is inside you. It will save you.

He turns his head. The clock reads 5:43. Beth is still asleep, turned away from him, her breathing slow and peaceful.

In a few hours, he has to sit in Father John's office and explain what's happening to him.

He doesn't know if he can.

But the waitress's words echo in him: *What you keep inside will destroy you.*

And the homeless man's eyes: *You've been a passerby your whole life.*

He lies there, watching the light grow stronger, carrying two more encounters inside him now. Five visitations. Five teachings.

The kingdom is spread out upon the earth.

Why do you hold so tightly to what washes away?

Split a piece of wood. I am there.

Whatever you did for the least of these, you did for me.

Bring forth what is inside you.

He has to speak. He has to tell someone. He has to *bring it forth.*

Today. Father John.

He doesn't know if the priest will believe him. He doesn't know if anyone will. But the words are pressing against his chest now, demanding release, and he understands, finally, fully, that silence is no longer an option.

The truth wants to be spoken.

And he is the one who must speak it.

Chapter Ten

Father John

The drive to the church is quiet.

Beth is behind the wheel, the way she was on Sunday. Lem sits in the passenger seat, watching the familiar roads slide past. The hardware store. The waterfront. The oak-lined street that leads to St. Paul's.

Everything looks the same. Everything is different.

"You okay?" Beth asks.

"Yeah."

She glances at him. He can feel her studying his profile, searching for something, cracks, maybe. Signs of the breakdown she's been expecting.

But he's not breaking. Not today. Something has settled in him since last night: since the dock, since Mike's, since the waitress took his hand and told him to bring forth what was inside. The fear is still there, somewhere deep, but it's not running the show anymore.

He's going to tell the truth. That's all. Just tell the truth and let it land where it lands.

"You don't have to do this alone," Beth says. "I'll be right there with you."

He nods. He knows she loves him. But he also knows that she's hoping Father John will fix him. That the priest will say something wise, something pastoral, something that will make sense of the past week and return her husband to her, whole and reasonable and sane.

She doesn't understand that there's no going back. He's not the man he was before the dreams started. That man is gone. Whoever he's becoming, whoever he's being shaped into, that's who will walk into Father John's office today.

They pull into the parking lot. The church looks the same as it always has: white clapboard, modest steeple, the stained glass windows catching the December light.

Lem gets out of the car. Stands there a moment, looking at the building.

This is where he was married. Where Kate was baptized, his father's hands pouring the water while Father John assisted, both priests speaking the words over the infant in Lem's arms. Where he's knelt at the communion rail a thousand times, receiving the bread and wine, speaking the ancient words.

This is where he wept on Sunday, undone by the liturgy, overwhelmed by the sudden knowledge that someone was listening.

This is where Father John's hand trembled as he placed the wafer in Lem's palm, something passing between them that neither of them could name.

Lem takes a breath. Walks toward the door.

* * *

Father John had not slept well since Sunday.

Three nights now. Three nights of lying in the dark, staring at the ceiling of the rectory, replaying the moment at the communion rail. Three nights of trying to pray and finding the words hollow in his mouth. Three nights of asking God for clarity and receiving only silence.

He sat at his desk now, waiting for the Robersons to arrive, his hands folded in front of him. The hands that had trembled on Sunday. The hands that had held the wafer over Lem's open palm and felt something move through him that he couldn't explain.

Forty years a priest. Forty years of standing at the altar, speaking the ancient words, believing, truly believing, that something sacred happened in the bread and wine. He had felt the presence, or thought he did. The quiet warmth during the Eucharist. The peace that sometimes settled over him in prayer. The sense that God was near, was listening, was pleased.

But always mediated. Always gentle. Always within the bounds of what he expected, what he was trained for, what the liturgy prepared him to receive.

What happened with Lem was different.

Father John closed his eyes, and it was there again, the memory he couldn't escape. The communion line moving forward, face after face, the motions automatic after so many years. Margaret Wilson. Frank Simmons. The Peterson children, fidgeting even as they received. And then Lem, kneeling at the rail, his face still damp with tears he hadn't bothered to wipe.

Father John had administered communion thousands of times. The motions were muscle memory now: the wafer held aloft, the words spoken, the bread placed in the open palm. Sacred, yes. He believed that. But also routine. The mystery contained, controlled, channeled through the liturgy the way it had been channeled for two thousand years.

But when Lem looked up, when their eyes met, something happened that wasn't in the rubrics.

It was communion. But not the kind Father John was administering. This moved the other direction. *Through* Lem. *From* Lem. As if the Christ Father John invoked every Sunday was suddenly present in the man kneeling before him, looking back at him, *seeing* him.

His hand trembled. The wafer hovered over Lem's open palm. And for a moment, just a moment, Father John felt what the disciples must have felt on the road to Emmaus. The stranger breaking bread. The sudden recognition. *It's you. It's been you all along.*

A power he had never experienced. A presence he had prayed for his entire vocation but never truly expected to encounter, not like this, not through a parishioner, not in a form he couldn't control or contain.

Then the moment passed. Lem was just Lem again: the fisherman, the writer, the man who sat in the third pew from the back every Sunday for thirty years. The wafer fell into his palm. The words came out, hoarse but audible. "The Body of Christ, the bread of heaven."

But Father John knew. Something had happened that he couldn't explain, couldn't contain, couldn't fit inside forty years of priesthood.

God had shown up. And He hadn't used the approved channels.

Father John opened his eyes. Looked around his office: the books on the shelves, the crucifix on the wall, the window overlooking the cemetery where generations of this town lay buried. All the trappings of his vocation. All the structures he had built his life around.

What did any of it mean, if God could simply... show up? In a fisherman's eyes? Without warning, without ritual, without the careful mediation of the church?

He had prayed for this. That was the terrible irony. All his life, he had prayed to truly encounter God, not just the quiet warmth, not just the gentle peace, but the real thing. The burning bush. The still small voice. The road to Damascus.

And now it had happened. Or something had happened. And instead of falling to his knees in gratitude, he was terrified.

Because if Lem was telling the truth, if Christ was actually visiting him, speaking to him, appearing in his dreams, then everything Father John thought he understood about his own priesthood was called into question. Forty years of standing at the altar, and he had never experienced what Lem experienced on a fishing boat at dawn.

What did that make him? A fraud? A failure? A man who had spent his life going through the motions while the real thing passed him by?

Or just human. Just a man. A priest, yes, but still flesh and blood, still limited, still unable to receive what he wasn't ready to receive.

He heard the car pull into the parking lot. Heard the doors open and close. Heard footsteps approaching.

Father John straightened in his chair. Composed his face. Became, once again, the priest: calm, pastoral, in control.

He would do what the church trained him to do. He would listen. He would assess. He would recommend the prudent course of action.

He would not, could not, admit what he had felt at the communion rail.

Not yet. Maybe not ever.

* * *

Father John's office is in the parish hall, a small room lined with books and smelling faintly of old wood and candle wax. A single window looks out on the cemetery: the old stones, the newer ones, the generations of this town laid to rest in the shadow of the church.

He rises as Lem and Beth enter, comes around the desk to greet them. He is wearing his collar but no vestments: just a black shirt, gray slacks, the uniform of a priest on a weekday afternoon.

"Lem. Elizabeth. Thank you for coming."

He shakes Lem's hand. The grip is firm, but something in it is careful. Watchful. He can't quite meet Lem's eyes, not yet. Not after Sunday.

"Please, sit."

There are two chairs arranged in front of the desk. Lem and Beth take them. Father John returns to his seat, settling into the worn leather, folding his hands on the desk in front of him.

For a moment, no one speaks.

Father John looks at Lem, really looks, for the first time since Sunday. This man he has known for thirty years. This man whose wedding he blessed, whose hand he has shaken at the church door a thousand times. He remembers Kate as a child, serious and attentive, carrying the cross down the aisle in her acolyte robes. Remembers her voice rising with the choir on Easter morning. Remembers the day she left for college, how Lem and Beth had sat in this very office, proud and grieving in equal measure, asking Father John to pray for her.

He has been part of this family. Not by blood, but by presence. Thirty years of baptisms and funerals, of hospital visits and holiday dinners, of being there when he was needed.

And now Lem is sitting across from him, waiting to tell him something that will test everything between them.

"I've been worried about you," Father John says finally. "Since Sunday. Since I saw you in the service."

Lem nods. "I know."

"Elizabeth called me Monday morning. Told me what's been happening. The sleeplessness. The... disturbance." He pauses, choosing his words carefully. "She's concerned. So am I."

"I understand."

Father John studies him. Looking for cracks. Looking for signs. Looking for anything that will let him believe this is a medical problem, a psychological break, something that can be diagnosed and treated and contained.

But Lem's eyes are clear. His voice is steady. He looks, if anything, more present than Father John has ever seen him. More *here*.

That is the most frightening thing of all.

"Tell me what's been happening, Lem. In your own words."

Lem looks at Beth. She gives him a small nod, her eyes bright with hope. She thinks this is the right thing. She thinks Father John can help.

Lem turns back to the priest.

"I've been having dreams," he says.

His voice is steady. Calm. Father John watches him speak, the way the words come out simply, clearly, without the hesitation or confusion you'd expect from someone in the grip of delusion.

"Not regular dreams. Something else. They started about a week ago. They feel... different. More real than real. More vivid. And they don't fade when I wake up. I can see them still. Every detail."

Father John listens. His face gives nothing away, but inside, something is tightening. He knows where this is going. Has known since Sunday.

"What happens in these dreams?"

Lem takes a breath.

"Someone visits me. Someone I recognize, even though he looks different each time. A stranger on my boat. A child on the shore. A man mending nets on the dock behind the fish house. A homeless man on the waterfront. A waitress at Mike's."

He pauses. Father John is very still.

"They speak to me. They say things, things I've never heard before, but feel true. Feel more true than anything I've ever been told in my life."

"What kind of things?"

Lem meets his eyes. And Father John feels it again, that flicker, that presence, that sense of something larger looking back at him through Lem's gaze.

"'The kingdom of the Father is spread out upon the earth, and people do not see it.' 'Split a piece of wood; I am there. Lift a shell, and you will find me.' 'Whatever you did for the least of these, you did for me.' 'Bring forth what is inside you, it's the only thing that saves.'"

Father John's face flickers. He can't help it. The words landed in him with a force he wasn't prepared for. He knows some of them, the Gospel of Matthew, the teaching about the least of these. But the others... *Split a piece of driftwood; I am there.* He has never heard that. It sounds ancient. It sounds true.

"And at the end of each dream," Lem continues, "just before I wake, I see his face. The real face. Always the same, no matter what form he's taken. Always the same eyes."

The room is very quiet. Outside, a bird is singing in the cemetery. The December light falls through the window, casting long shadows on the bookshelves.

"Who do you see, Lem?" Father John asks. His voice is low. Careful. He already knows the answer. Has known it since Sunday, when those eyes looked up at him from the communion rail. "Who do you think is visiting you in these dreams?"

Lem holds his gaze. He isn't going to flinch. Isn't going to soften it or hedge it or make it easier to dismiss.

"I think it's Christ," he says. "I think Jesus Christ has been visiting me in my dreams."

Beside him, Beth draws a sharp breath. Father John doesn't look at her. He keeps his eyes on Lem.

The words hang in the air. The truth, or madness, spoken plainly.

And Father John feels it again. That presence. That power. The same thing he felt at the communion rail, moving through Lem like light through a window. For a moment, he wants to fall on his knees. Wants to weep. Wants to say, *I know, I felt it too, I believe you.*

But he doesn't.

He can't.

Because admitting that Lem is telling the truth would mean admitting that everything Father John thinks he understands about God, about how He works, how He appears, what He asks, is incomplete. Would mean admitting that forty years of careful priesthood, of controlled sacraments, of approved channels for the divine, are just one small piece of something much larger.

And he isn't ready for that. Isn't brave enough. Isn't faithful enough.

He is only human.

"I know how it sounds," Lem continues. "I know it sounds like I'm losing my mind. I've asked myself that question a hundred times. I've lain awake at night wondering if I'm having a breakdown. If the stress finally cracked something in me. If I need to be medicated or hospitalized or just... stopped."

He shakes his head slowly.

"But I don't believe that. I've tried to believe it, it would be easier if I could. But I know what I've experienced. It's more real than this room. More real than this conversation. And the things he's said to me, they're not the ravings of a broken mind. They're true. I know they're true the way I know the water and the sky and my own name."

He falls silent. The truth is out now, sitting in the middle of Father John's office like a living thing.

Beth is crying quietly. Father John can hear her breathing, the small catches as she tries to hold it together. Lem reaches over without looking and takes her hand. She grips it tight.

Father John is silent for a long moment. His hands are still folded on the desk, but they are pressed together harder now. The knuckles white.

He knows what he should say. Knows what his heart is crying out to say:

I believe you. I felt it too. Tell me everything.

But his training speaks louder. His fear speaks louder. The institution he has served for forty years rises up in him like a wall, and he takes shelter behind it.

When he speaks, his voice is measured. Pastoral. The voice of a priest who has had training in these situations.

"Lem, I want you to know that I take what you're saying seriously. I don't dismiss it. The church has a long history of visions, of mystical experiences, of encounters with the divine. The saints themselves often described experiences not unlike what you're describing."

He pauses. Lem waits.

"But the church is also cautious about these things. Very cautious. Because the mind is complex, and the unconscious can create experiences that feel absolutely real, more real than waking life, but that are, in fact, products of stress, or grief, or unprocessed trauma."

"You think I'm imagining it."

"I think you're experiencing something powerful and real to you. I don't doubt that for a moment. What I'm less certain about is the *source* of that experience. Whether it's truly... external. Or whether it's arising from within, from places in yourself that you haven't fully examined."

The words taste like ashes in his mouth. He knows they are wrong even as he speaks them. Knows he is betraying something, Lem, the truth, his own vocation. But he can't stop. The fear is too strong.

Lem nods slowly. His face shows no anger. Only a kind of sad understanding.

"What are you suggesting?"

Father John glances at Beth, then back at Lem.

"I think it would be wise to speak with someone. A professional. Someone trained in these matters, someone who can help you process what you're experiencing and determine whether there might be... underlying causes."

The word hangs in the air. *Underlying causes.* Medical causes. Psychological causes. A diagnosis that would explain everything, wrap it up in a neat clinical package, and make it safe.

Make it containable. Make it go away.

Lem looks at Beth. Her face is hopeful now, relieved. This is what she wants. A path forward. A solution. A way to get her husband back.

He looks at Father John.

And Father John sees that Lem *knew.*

The fisherman's eyes hold his, steady, unblinking, full of something that looks like compassion. Not anger. Not accusation. Just a clear-eyed recognition of what is happening.

Lem sees right through him. Sees the fear. Sees the retreat. Sees the priest who felt the power of the Spirit at the communion rail and is now sending that same Spirit to a psychiatrist.

And still, there is no judgment in his eyes. Only sorrow.

That is worse than anger. Far worse.

"Thank you, Father," Lem says.

Father John looks up, surprised by the abrupt close. "Lem, I hope you understand, this isn't a judgment. It's concern. It's pastoral care. We want to help you."

"I know."

He does know. Father John can see it. Lem understands, understands that the priest cares about him, understands that the recommendation comes from something other than malice. And that understanding, that grace, makes Father John's failure all the more bitter.

"I'll think about what you've said," Lem says.

He helps Beth to her feet. She is still holding his hand, still gripping tight. She looks at him with a question in her eyes: *Are you okay? Are you going to do what he says?*

He doesn't answer. Not yet.

"Lem." Father John has risen too. His voice is unsteady now, the pastoral composure cracking. "I want you to know... whatever is happening to you, you're not alone. The church is here for you. I'm here for you."

The words sound hollow even as he speaks them. *I'm here for you.* He has just sent the man to a psychiatrist. What kind of "here" is that?

Lem meets his eyes. Holds them for a long moment. And in that gaze, Father John sees something that will haunt him for days afterward: not reproach, but invitation. As if Lem is giving him one last chance to step forward, to admit what he felt, to join him in whatever is happening.

Father John can't do it. His feet are rooted to the floor. His mouth won't form the words.

The moment passes.

"I know," Lem says again. "Thank you."

He turns. Walks to the door. Beth follows.

As he reaches the threshold, he stops. Looks back.

Father John is standing behind his desk, hands at his sides, his face a mask of pastoral concern. But the mask is slipping now. And beneath it, in the eyes, in the set of the jaw, something else is visible.

Fear. The fear of a man who has glimpsed something too large for his categories.

And beneath the fear, something that looks almost like longing. The longing of a man who has prayed his whole life for an encounter with God, and who has just turned away from one.

Lem nods once. A small gesture, almost imperceptible. *I understand. I forgive you. I'll be here when you're ready.*

Then he walks out of the office, out of the parish hall, out into the December afternoon.

Father John stands alone in his office, surrounded by his books and his crucifix and his forty years of priesthood.

He has done the right thing. The prudent thing. The thing his training demanded.

So why does he feel like Peter, standing in the courtyard, hearing the rooster crow?

* * *

They sit in the car for a long time before Beth starts the engine.

Lem stares out the window at the church. The white clapboard. The modest steeple. The stained glass windows where he once saw Christ looking back at him.

"He's right, you know," Beth says finally. Her voice is gentle, careful. "It might help to talk to someone. A professional. Someone who can..."

She trails off. She doesn't know how to finish the sentence.

"Someone who can explain it away," Lem says quietly.

"That's not what I..."

"I'm not angry, Beth. I understand. I know you're scared. I know you want your husband back."

She is crying again. Silently, the tears streaming down her face.

"I *am* your husband," he says. "I'm still here. I'm just... different now. Something's happened to me, and I can't unhappen it. I can't go back to who I was before."

"But what if Father John is right? What if there's something wrong, something medical, and we could fix it? Wouldn't you want to know?"

He turns to look at her. This woman he has loved for thirty years. This woman who has stood beside him through everything. This woman who is looking at him now with hope and fear in equal measure.

"There's nothing to fix," he says gently. "I'm not broken. I'm being changed."

She doesn't understand. He can see it in her face. She wants to understand, wants desperately to believe him, but she can't. The distance between them is the distance between someone who has seen and someone who hasn't. There's no bridge across that gap. Not yet.

"Let's go home," he says.

She wipes her eyes. Nods. Starts the engine.

They drive home in silence.

* * *

That night, Lem sits on the dock alone.

The water is black and still. The stars are bright overhead, winter stars, clear and cold. Duke lies beside him, head on paws, keeping watch.

He thinks about Father John. The careful words. The pastoral concern. The flicker in his eyes that betrayed what he really felt.

He saw it, the moment when Father John almost stepped forward. Almost admitted what he felt at the communion rail. Almost chose faith over fear.

And then the moment passed, and the priest retreated behind his training, and the wall went up.

Lem doesn't blame him. He can't. He knows what it is like to be afraid of something too large to contain. Knows what it costs to speak truth that sounds like madness. Father John has spent forty years building a house for God to live in. And now God has shown up outside the house, and the priest doesn't know what to do.

That is human. That is forgivable.

Lem hopes Father John will find his way. Hopes the longing he saw beneath the fear will eventually win out. Hopes that someday, the priest will knock on his door and say *I believe you. I felt it too. Tell me everything.*

He thinks about Beth. The hope on her face when Father John made his recommendation. The relief at having a path forward, a solution, a way to make sense of the senseless.

She loves him. That is the thing he holds onto. She loves him, and she is afraid, and she is doing the only thing she knows how to do: reaching for the structures that have always held her: the church, the doctor, the diagnosis.

He thinks about Kate. He should call her, has promised he would. But the words won't come. Not yet.

The teachings move through him, unbidden:

The kingdom is spread out upon the earth.

Why do you hold so tightly to what washes away?

Split a piece of wood. I am there.

Whatever you did for the least of these, you did for me.

Bring forth what is inside you.

He brought it forth. He spoke the truth. And the priest heard it the way a doctor hears a symptom.

Maybe that's all it is. Maybe Father John is right. Maybe there's something broken in him that a professional could name, could treat, could fix.

He waits for that possibility to settle into relief.

It doesn't.

The dreams are still there, vivid, undimmed, more real than the boards beneath him. The faces. The words. The eyes that are always the same, no matter what form they wear.

He doesn't know what to do with any of it. Doesn't know what is being asked of him. Doesn't know if he is strong enough to carry it, or wise enough to understand it, or brave enough to speak it again after today.

He only knows he can't unsee what he's seen.

He can't unhear what he's heard.

And somewhere beneath the fear, beneath the confusion, beneath the loneliness of being the only one who knows what he knows, there is something else. Something that feels less like certainty and more like gravity. A weight that won't let him turn away.

More dreams are coming. He can feel it the way he can feel weather building on the water.

He doesn't know what they'll bring. Doesn't know what they'll ask.

He sits on the dock, his dog beside him, the stars wheeling slowly overhead.

Waiting.

Chapter Eleven

The Gallery

He doesn't remember entering.

One moment he is somewhere else, home, maybe, or the space between sleep and waking where dreams have not yet taken shape, and then he is here. Standing in a room of white walls and polished concrete floors. A gallery. Small. Nearly empty. The kind of place that exists in cities he rarely visits, in neighborhoods where people drink wine from glasses without stems and speak in low voices about things that matter only to them.

He doesn't belong here. He knows that immediately. His boots are wrong. His hands are wrong, calloused, salt-cracked, the hands of a man who works lines and nets, not a man who contemplates art.

But he's here.

The room is silent except for one sound: a faint rhythm, steady and low. It takes him a moment to recognize it. A heartbeat. Not his own, or maybe his own, amplified, externalized, filling the white space like a pulse.

There is only one painting.

It hangs on the far wall, large, maybe six feet across. He walks toward it without deciding to walk. His boots make no sound on the concrete.

The painting is... he doesn't have words for what the painting is.

Color, first. Deep blues and golds, layered thick, almost sculptural. A landscape, maybe. Or a figure. Or both. The longer he looks, the less certain he becomes. There's a horizon line that could be water or sky. There's a shape at the center that could be a person or a door or a wound.

It shifts.

He blinks. The colors have rearranged themselves. The gold has moved. The figure, if it is a figure, has turned.

He steps closer. The heartbeat grows louder.

"It does that."

The voice comes from beside him. He turns.

A woman stands there. He doesn't know how long she's been there, seconds, hours, the whole time. She's middle-aged, maybe sixty, with gray hair pulled back and eyes that hold more than her face shows. She's looking at the painting, not at him.

"Does what?" he asks.

"Changes. Depending on who's looking. Depending on what they need to see."

He looks back at the canvas. The blues have deepened. The shape at the center has opened, or closed. He can't tell which.

"That can't be real," he says.

"No," she agrees. "It isn't."

They stand together in silence. The heartbeat continues, steady, patient. He realizes he's breathing in rhythm with it.

"I've seen you before," he says. The words come out before he can stop them. He doesn't know if they're true. But something in her, the way she holds her head, the stillness of her hands, is familiar in a way that goes deeper than memory.

"You've seen me many times," she says. "You just didn't know what you were looking at."

She turns to face him. Her eyes are dark, ancient, lit from within by something that doesn't come from the gallery's soft lighting.

"That's always the problem, isn't it?" she continues. "You see, but you don't recognize. You look, but you don't understand what you're looking at."

"I don't..."

"The fisherman on your boat. The child on the beach. The old man with the net. The waitress at Mike's. The man on the bench." She tilts her head slightly. "Did you think those were different visitors?"

His chest tightens. The heartbeat in the room is his heartbeat now, he feels it pounding in his throat, his temples, the center of his palms.

"They felt different," he manages. "They looked..."

"They looked like what you could bear to see."

She gestures toward the painting. The colors are swirling now, slow as honey, rearranging themselves into something almost recognizable: a face, a hand, a shoreline, gone.

"Truth doesn't come into the world naked," she says. "It never has. It comes in types and images. In forms you can hold. Shapes you can approach."

She steps closer to the canvas. Her reflection appears in the glass, but it's not her reflection. It's his. Or no, it's neither of them. It's someone else entirely. A figure of light. A shape without features. A presence.

"The world will not receive truth any other way," she says. "This is not deception. This is mercy."

"Mercy," he repeats. The word feels strange in his mouth.

"If it came to you unveiled..." She turns back to him, and her eyes are not eyes anymore. They are windows. They are wells. They are the place where light begins. "If you saw the full truth, unmediated, unhidden, you would be destroyed. Not from cruelty. From radiance. From the weight of what is."

He wants to step back. He can't move.

"The images are how I come to those I love," she says. "The fisherman. The child. The waitress at the diner. These are not masks. They are kindness. They are the only way I can reach you without it consuming you."

The painting behind her has stopped shifting. It has resolved into something: a figure, standing at the edge of the world, arms open, face obscured by light.

"You keep asking why it comes this way," she says. "In forms you almost recognize. In voices that feel familiar but not quite. You keep asking why you can't see clearly."

She reaches toward him. Not touching, just reaching. The air between her hand and his chest grows warm.

"But you are seeing clearly. You're seeing exactly what you're able to see. And each time, you see a little more. Each dream, the veil thins. Each visitation, you grow stronger."

"Stronger for what?" he whispers.

She smiles. It's the saddest smile he's ever seen. The most joyful. Both at once.

"For what comes next."

The heartbeat stops.

The silence is absolute, a silence so complete it has texture, weight, presence. The painting dissolves into light. The walls fade. The woman's form begins to blur, to radiate, to become something his eyes cannot hold.

She speaks one more time. Her lips don't move. The words arrive directly in his chest, in his blood, in the place where he keeps the truths he's never told anyone:

When you see what is real, truly real, you will not be the same. No one who sees can remain unchanged. But do not be afraid. The light that transforms is the light that loves. They are the same light.

Her face begins to clarify. The features sharpening. The eyes becoming specific, known, unmistakable...

He wakes.

* * *

The bedroom is dark. Beth is breathing beside him, deep in her own sleep. The clock reads 3:47.

He lies still, staring at the ceiling. His chest is warm, not fever-warm, but warm like sunlight, like a hand has rested there and only just lifted away.

The woman's words echo in him: *The images are how I come to those I love.*

He thinks of all the faces. The fisherman. The child. The old man. The waitress. The homeless man.

Different faces. The same eyes.

He understands now. Not fully, he's not sure he'll ever understand fully, but enough. Enough to stop asking why. Enough to start asking what's next.

He closes his eyes. The warmth in his chest remains.

For the first time in weeks, he doesn't dread the morning.

Chapter Twelve

The Phone Call

Friday morning comes gray and soft.

Lem wakes with the warmth still in his chest, faint now but present. Beth is already up, he can hear her moving in the kitchen, the clink of a mug, the soft shuffle of her slippers on the hardwood.

He lies still for a moment, looking at the ceiling. The dream is with him. The woman in the gallery. The painting that shifted. The words that arrived without sound: *The images are how I come to those I love.*

He understands something now that he didn't understand before. Not everything, but something. A piece of the architecture. A reason for the forms.

He gets up. Showers. Dresses. The day feels ordinary in a way that's almost disorienting after the night. The world just going on: coffee brewing, light strengthening, the bay flat and silver through the bedroom window.

He needs to check the boat. The bilge pump was running more than it should last time he was out. Probably just the float switch, but he should look at it.

He walks down the hall toward the kitchen, already thinking about the boat, about the tools he'll need, about whether Bud might want to come out later...

And stops.

Beth's voice. Low. The particular tone she uses when she's trying not to be overheard.

"...haven't slept through the night in a week. I lie there listening to him breathe, and I don't even know if he's really sleeping or just somewhere else. Somewhere in those dreams."

Not Beth. Kate. The response comes through the phone on the counter, on speaker. Kate's voice filling the kitchen.

"Have you talked to him? Really talked?"

"I've tried. He tries too, I can see him trying. But it's like there's a wall of glass between us. He's right there, right in front of me, and I can't reach him."

Lem stands in the hallway, just out of sight. He should announce himself. Should walk in, pour his coffee, let them know he's there.

He doesn't move.

"Mom, I need to ask you something, and I need you to be honest with me." Kate's voice has shifted, it's her professional voice now, the one she uses with patients and families. Lem has heard it before, on the rare occasions he's called her at work. Clinical. Careful. "Has Dad shown any other symptoms? Headaches? Visual disturbances? Changes in his sense of smell?"

"What? No. I don't think so. Why?"

"Because what he's describing, the vividness of the dreams, the way they persist after waking, the emotional intensity, the sense of presence, in my world, that pattern has a differential diagnosis. Temporal lobe involvement. Seizure activity. Early neurodegenerative changes."

"Katie..."

"I'm not saying that's what it is. I'm saying I can't stop my brain from going there. I'm trained to look for organic causes. I can't turn it off, even when it's my own father."

A pause. The sound of Beth's mug being set down.

"When I was on the boat with him," Kate continues, "I looked in his eyes and I believed him. I *knew* he wasn't delusional. He was oriented, coherent, emotionally appropriate. Everything I'm trained to assess, it all checked out. But now, back here, back in the hospital every day seeing what I see..."

"You're having doubts."

"I'm having doubts about my doubts. I don't know what I know anymore, Mom. I believed him. I still want to believe him. But what if believing him means missing something treatable? What if I'm so desperate for my father to be special that I let something slip by that could kill him?"

Lem feels the words land in his chest. Not anger, not yet. Something colder. The recognition of distance opening.

"Father John recommended a psychiatrist," Beth says. Her voice is tired. Worn down to the bone. "Lem just thanked him and walked out. He wasn't rude about it, you know your father, he's never rude, but he wasn't going to do it. I could see it in his face."

"What did Father John say exactly? About what he felt at the communion rail?"

"He didn't say much. He looked shaken, really shaken, Katie, like something had happened to him too. But when I asked, he retreated into priest-talk. 'The church is careful about these things.' 'We should rule out medical causes.' He was kind about it, but..." Beth's voice drops. "He thinks your father is having some kind of breakdown. I could see it in his eyes."

"Maybe he's right." Kate's voice is smaller now. The physician retreating, the daughter emerging. "Maybe there's something we're missing. A tumor. An aneurysm. Something that could be treated before..."

She doesn't finish. She doesn't have to.

"I've thought about that." Beth's voice cracks. "God help me, I've thought about it every night. Part of me *wants* it to be a tumor. Because a tumor I could understand. A tumor has a treatment plan. A tumor is something the doctors can see on a scan and point to and say *there, that's the problem, we can fix that.*"

"Mom..."

"But what if it's not a tumor, Katie? What if there's nothing wrong with his brain? What if..." Beth stops. When she speaks again, her voice is barely above a whisper. "What if he's telling the truth?"

Silence. The refrigerator hums. Somewhere outside, a gull cries.

"I've sat in that pew next to your father for thirty years." Beth's words come slowly now, pulled from somewhere deep. "Every Sunday. His hand in mine during the prayers. Our voices together on the hymns. I thought I knew what faith was. I thought I understood how God works: through the church, through the sacraments, through the rituals I've practiced my whole life."

"Mom, you don't have to..."

"But what if I was wrong? What if God is bigger than St. Paul's? Bigger than the liturgy? What if He shows up on fishing boats and in dreams and in ways the church doesn't have a category for?" Her voice breaks completely. "What if my husband is experiencing something real, something *holy*, and I'm sitting here wishing it was a tumor because a tumor would be easier to accept?"

Lem closes his eyes. His hand finds the wall. Steadies him.

He's heard Beth pray. Every night, for thirty years, the soft murmur of her voice beside him in the dark, the familiar words rising and falling like breath. He's always loved that about her. The steadiness of it. The faith that didn't need to be dramatic to be real.

He didn't know it was costing her this much. Didn't know she was lying awake, torn between the faith she knew and the thing she was witnessing.

"I don't know what to tell you, Mom." Kate's voice is raw now. No more physician's distance. Just a daughter, frightened for her parents, caught between worlds. "I sat on that boat and I believed him. I felt something, I don't know what to call it, but I felt it. And then I came back here, back to the hospital, back to my life, and the doubt crept in. Because what he's describing doesn't fit anything I was taught. Not in medical school. Not in church. Not anywhere."

"I know."

"But I also know Dad. I've known him my whole life. He taught me to fish. He raised me in that pew. He showed up every single day, every recital, every game, every moment that mattered. He's the most grounded person I've ever known. He doesn't make things up. He doesn't imagine things. He's not looking for attention or validation or any of the things that would explain this."

"I know."

"So either my father, the sanest man I know, is having a psychotic break that presents in a way I've never seen in my training... or something is actually happening to him that I don't have a framework for. And I don't know which one scares me more."

Beth doesn't respond right away. When she does, her voice is thick with tears.

"I love him so much, Katie. That's what makes this so hard. Thirty years of loving him. Thirty years of building a life together. I know the sound of his breathing when he's worried. I know the way he holds his coffee when he's thinking. I know every line on his face, every mood, every silence." She takes a shaky breath. "And now he's somewhere I can't follow. And I don't know how to love him there. I don't know how to reach him."

"I know, Mom. I love him too."

"He's not crazy. I know that much. Whatever else I don't know, I know that. Your father is not crazy."

"Then what is he?"

The question hangs in the air. Neither of them answers.

"Should I come back down?" Kate asks finally. "I can rearrange my schedule. I can be there tonight if you need me."

"No. Not yet. I don't want him to feel like we're... managing him. Circling him like he's a problem to be solved."

"We're not..."

"I know we're not. But that's how it would feel to him. If you showed up again, out of the blue, right after Father John recommended a psychiatrist..." Beth sighs. "He'd know we'd been talking. He'd feel ambushed."

"You're probably right."

"I just want him back, Katie. I want him to be okay. I want..."

Her voice gives out.

"I know, Mom. I want that too."

"I'm going to keep praying. That's all I know how to do. Keep showing up. Keep loving him. And pray that God shows me how to be what he needs, even if I don't understand what's happening."

"That's not nothing, Mom. That's a lot."

"It doesn't feel like enough."

"I know. But it's what we have."

Another pause. Lem can hear Beth moving, the creak of the kitchen stool, the soft sound of her wiping her face.

"I should go," Kate says. "I've got rounds in twenty minutes. But call me, okay? Anytime. Day or night. If anything changes, if you need me, I'm there."

"I know, sweetheart. I love you."

"I love you too, Mom. And tell Dad... no, don't tell him anything. Just... love him. That's all any of us can do."

"I will."

The call ends. The kitchen goes quiet.

Lem stands frozen in the hallway.

Kate. His Katie. Who sat across from him on the boat and looked him in the eye. Who said *I don't think you're crazy. I believe YOU.* Who held his hand and didn't flinch.

Kate. Running differentials in her head. Thinking about temporal lobes and tumors. Wondering if she's missing something treatable while her father slips away.

She's not wrong to wonder. He sees that now. She's a physician, it's her job to consider organic causes, to rule out the medical before accepting the miraculous. She's not betraying him by thinking like a doctor. She's loving him the only way she knows how.

And Beth. His Beth. Thirty years of marriage, thirty years of showing up, and she's lying awake at night wondering if her faith is big enough to hold what's happening to him. Praying for God to show her the way. Wishing it was a tumor because a tumor would be easier to love.

They're afraid because they love him. Kate reached for "tumor" because her training is how she loves, by diagnosing, by treating, by fixing. Beth reached for Father John because her faith is how she loves, through the church, through the rituals, through the approved channels.

They're trying to save him. They just don't understand that he doesn't need saving.

The warmth in his chest is gone. In its place, something cold. Something heavy. Not anger, something worse. The recognition that even love has limits. That the people who love him most are the ones who can't follow where he's going.

He turns. Walks back down the hall. Past the bedroom. Past the bathroom. Through the living room. He takes his keys from the hook by the door. Slips on his boots.

Duke raises his head from his bed, tail thumping once.

"Stay, boy," Lem murmurs.

He opens the door. Steps out into the gray morning. The air is cool and damp, carrying the smell of salt and marsh.

His truck is in the driveway. He gets in. Starts the engine.

Through the kitchen window, he can see Beth. Still at the counter. Her face in her hands now. Shoulders shaking.

She's crying.

He almost goes back in. Almost takes her in his arms, tells her everything is going to be okay.

But he doesn't know if it's going to be okay. He only knows it's going to be different. And he doesn't have words for that. Not yet.

He backs out of the driveway. Pulls onto the road.

He doesn't know where he's going. The marina, maybe. The water. Somewhere he can breathe. Somewhere the silence isn't full of the sound of the people he loves trying to diagnose him back to normal.

The house shrinks in his rearview mirror. Beth at the window now, watching him go.

He drives.

Chapter Thirteen

Bud

The marina is quiet this morning.

Lem pulls into the gravel lot and sits for a moment, hands on the wheel, engine idling. A few pickups scattered near the dock. A pelican on a piling. The sound of halyards clinking against masts in the light breeze.

He should go home. Should walk back into that kitchen, tell Beth he heard, have the conversation that needs to happen.

He can't.

Not yet. Not with Kate's voice still in his ears. *Maybe there's something medical. A tumor.*

His daughter. His Katie. The one who believed him on the boat, who looked him in the eye and said *I believe YOU.* Now running differentials in her head. Now wondering if her father's brain is betraying him.

He pulls out his phone. Finds Bud's number. Types a message:

You want to go out?

The reply comes in less than a minute:

Give me ten.

* * *

Bud's boat is the old Sea Ox he rebuilt himself years ago, the kind of boat the Downeast boys run, nothing fancy, just a solid hull and an outboard that starts when you need it to. Lem helps him load the cooler, check the fuel, cast off the lines.

"Where to?" Bud asks, settling behind the wheel.

"Anywhere," Lem says. "Just out."

Bud nods. No questions. No curious looks. Just the ease of thirty-five years.

Thirty-five years. Lem lets that number settle over him as Bud backs out of the slip. They'd met the summer before Lem's junior year at Chapel Hill, two young men hauling shrimp nets on Captain Roy's boat, learning each other through the wordless language of shared labor. Bud had been born to this water, his people here for generations. Lem had come from Sullivan's Island, "from off" as the locals said, a college boy looking for something he couldn't name.

He'd found it. Found Bud. Found the Downeast community that would become his home. Found Beth, because Bud had introduced them, had seen something that August night at the fish camp and made it happen with nothing more than a nod and a "Beth, this is Lem."

Everything Lem had built in Beaufort traced back to this man. This friendship. This boat.

Bud threads through the no-wake zone and opens up the throttle once they clear the markers. The bow rises, then levels. The wind hits Lem's face. The shore falls away.

For a while, neither of them speaks. They don't need to. The years of friendship has taught them the value of silence: when to fill it, when to leave it alone.

They run south, past the marsh islands, past the oyster beds, past the old fish house where Captain Roy used to unload his catch. The water is calm, the sky still gray but brightening. A pair of ospreys circle over a stand of dead pines.

Bud cuts the engine near a grass flat they both know. The sudden quiet is immense: just the lap of water against the hull, the cry of gulls, the faint rustle of marsh grass in the breeze.

He opens the cooler. Hands Lem a bottle of water. Takes one for himself.

"You look like hell," he says.

"Thanks."

"I mean it. You sleeping?"

"Some."

Bud nods. Doesn't push. He picks up a rod, starts rigging a soft plastic, his fingers moving through the familiar motions. Those hands had done everything: hauled nets, built boats, dressed deer, pulled Lem out of more than one bad situation over the years. Hands that knew how to work, how to wait, how to hold on.

Lem watches the water. The light shifting on the surface. The kingdom spread out upon the earth.

"I need to tell you something," he says.

"Alright." Bud doesn't look up.

"It's going to sound crazy."

"Most things do."

Lem almost smiles. Almost. He picks up a rod from the rod holder. Starts rigging it. Something to do with his hands.

"I've been having dreams," he says. "For over a week now. Vivid ones. More real than any dream I've ever had."

He casts. Watches the lure arc out over the water, land softly, sink.

"There's always someone in them. A figure. Different forms: a fisherman, a child, an old man mending nets, a waitress, a homeless guy on a bench. Different every time. But the same."

"The same how?"

"The eyes. The voice. The... presence." He retrieves slowly, feeling the lure bump along the bottom. "They say things. Things I've never heard before but feel like I've always known. Things about seeing what's in front of you. About bringing forth what's inside. About the kingdom being here, spread out, and people not seeing it."

Bud casts his own line. Says nothing.

"Last night there was a woman in an art gallery. She told me why they come in different forms. Said if the truth came unveiled, if I saw it fully, I'd be destroyed. Said the images are mercy."

The words hang in the air between them. Lem reels in. Casts again.

"I told Beth. She thinks I'm losing my mind. I told Father John. He recommended a psychiatrist." He pauses. "I told Kate. On the boat, a few days ago. She said she believed me."

"And?"

"This morning I heard her on the phone with Beth. Talking about me. Wondering if it's a tumor. Something that could be treated."

Bud is quiet for a long moment. He reels in his line slowly, checking the lure, then casts again.

"What do you think it is?" he asks finally. "These dreams. These visitors."

Lem looks out at the water. The marsh. The sky. The world that looks exactly the same as it did a month ago and completely different.

"I think it's Christ," he says. "I think he's been visiting me. Teaching me. Preparing me for something."

He waits for Bud to laugh. To make a joke. To change the subject the way men do when things get too strange, too heavy, too real.

Bud doesn't laugh.

He reels in his line. Sets the rod down. Turns to look at Lem directly, the first time since they left the dock.

"I've known you since we were eighteen years old," he says. "Hauling shrimp on Captain Roy's boat. You were a college boy from off, didn't know your ass from a hole in the ground. But you worked harder than anybody I'd ever seen. Never complained. Never quit."

He takes a drink of water. Wipes his mouth with the back of his hand.

"Thirty-five years, Lem. That's longer than I've known anybody except my own blood. I was there when you married Beth. I was there when Kate was born. I was there when your daddy died and you couldn't hardly stand up straight for a week."

He sets the water bottle down. His eyes are steady on Lem's face.

"In all that time, you've never lied to me. Not once. You've never made things up. You've never been the guy who sees things that aren't there, believes things that don't make sense. You're the most level-headed son of a bitch I've ever known, and I still can't figure out how a man from off learned to read the water the way you do."

Lem says nothing. Waits.

"I don't go to church," Bud continues. "You know that. Haven't been since I was a kid. I don't know what God wants with anybody. Don't know if he wants anything at all."

He picks up his rod again. Holds it but doesn't cast.

"But if you tell me something's happening to you, if you tell me someone's visiting you in your dreams, teaching you things, I'm not gonna sit here and tell you you're crazy." He shakes his head slowly. "I don't understand it. Can't pretend I do. But I know you. And you're not making this up."

"Bud..."

"Let me finish." He turns back to the water. Casts. The lure sails out, lands, sinks. "If something chose you for this, if something out there, God or Christ or whatever you want to call it, if it decided you were the one to see these things, to hear these things... who the hell am I to say it's wrong?"

He retrieves slowly, eyes on the line.

"If God made you worthy of this, whatever this is... I'm not gonna be the one to reject it."

The words land in Lem's chest. Settle there. He feels something loosen, a knot he didn't know he was carrying. The isolation that closed around him in the hallway this morning, that tightened with every mile he drove, it cracks. Just slightly. Just enough.

"You believe me?" His voice is rough.

"I believe *you*." Bud glances at him. "That's all I've got. Hope that's enough."

Lem looks away. The marsh. The water. The ospreys still circling.

"Yeah," he says quietly. "That's enough."

They fish in silence for a while. The sun breaks through the clouds, turns the water gold. A redfish tails in the shallows twenty yards out, its copper back catching the light.

"What are you going to do?" Bud asks eventually.

"I don't know." Lem watches the redfish disappear into deeper water. "Something's coming. I can feel it. Something I need to be ready for."

"You need anything, you call me."

"I know."

"I mean it. Day or night. Whatever it is."

Lem nods. The knot loosens a little more.

They fish until the sun is high. They don't catch much. It doesn't matter.

When they finally pull back into the slip, Bud cuts the engine and they tie off in silence. Lem steps onto the dock.

"Same time next week?" Bud asks.

"Yeah," Lem says. "Same time."

Bud nods. Starts stowing gear.

Lem walks up the dock toward his truck. Halfway there, he stops. Turns back.

Bud is watching him. Standing in the Sea Ox, one hand on the console, the morning light falling on his weathered face. The friend who introduced him to his wife. The friend who never asked for anything and gave everything. The friend who just heard something impossible and didn't flinch.

"Bud."

"Yeah?"

"Thank you."

Bud holds his gaze for a moment. Then he nods, once, slow, and turns back to his work.

Lem walks to his truck. Gets in. Sits there for a moment before starting the engine.

The isolation isn't gone. But it has a crack in it now.

Someone believes.

Chapter Fourteen

Friday Night

L em doesn't go home until dark.

He drives the back roads for hours after leaving the marina, past the fish houses, past the old crab shedding operation that closed years ago, past the church where he was married. Not going anywhere. Just moving. Letting Bud's words settle.

If God made you worthy of this, whatever this is... I'm not going to be the one to reject it.

When he finally pulls into the driveway, the kitchen light is on. Beth's silhouette moves past the window. He sits in the truck for a long moment, hands on the wheel.

He should go in. Should tell her what he heard this morning. Should have the conversation.

But what would it change?

She's afraid. Kate's afraid. They love him, and their love has turned to fear, and fear makes people say things like *tumor* and *something that could be treated*.

He gets out. Walks inside.

Beth is at the sink, washing dishes. She turns when he enters, her face tight with worry that loosens into something else when she sees him, relief, maybe, or exhaustion.

"Where were you?"

"Out with Bud. On the water."

She nods. Turns back to the sink. The silence between them is thick, awkward, full of things neither of them knows how to say.

"I saved you a plate," she says. "It's in the fridge."

"Thanks."

He doesn't eat. He sits at the kitchen table while she finishes the dishes, while she wipes down the counters, while she moves through the small rituals of closing up the house for the night. They don't talk. There's too much to say, and no way to begin.

When she goes to bed, he stays in the kitchen. Stares out at the dark water. Thinks about Kate's voice. *Maybe there's something medical.*

He goes to bed late. Beth is already asleep, or pretending to be. He lies beside her in the dark, listening to her breathe, feeling the distance between them like a physical thing.

Sleep comes slowly.

And then...

A cemetery.

He knows immediately that he's dreaming, and knows just as immediately that this knowledge changes nothing. The dream is as real as the bed he's lying in, more real than the kitchen where he sat an hour ago.

The sky is overcast, heavy, the color of old pewter. The light is strange, the pale gray of late afternoon, or perhaps early morning. Impossible to tell. Time doesn't work the way it should.

The gravestones stretch out in every direction. Rows and rows of them, some old and weathered, some new and sharp-edged. But something is wrong. He walks closer to the nearest stone.

No name.

The face of the marker is blank. Smooth gray granite, unmarked, as if the chisel never touched it.

He moves to the next. Blank. The next. Blank.

Every stone in the cemetery. Hundreds of them. Thousands. All nameless. All empty. Markers for lives that left no record, deaths that no one remembered, griefs that belonged to no one.

He walks among them. The grass is wet beneath his feet. The air smells of rain and turned earth and something else, something older, like the inside of a church.

And then he sees her.

A woman, kneeling before one of the blank stones. Her back is to him. Her shoulders shake with weeping, not the quiet tears of resignation, but deep sobs that seem to come from somewhere beyond her body.

He approaches slowly. His footsteps make no sound.

"Ma'am?"

She doesn't turn. Doesn't acknowledge him. Just keeps weeping, her hands pressed against the blank stone as if she could push words into it through sheer grief.

"Ma'am, are you alright? Can I help you?"

Her sobs continue. But something else is happening. Her tears, he can see them now, catching the strange gray light, they're not falling down her face.

They're rising.

Droplets lifting from her cheeks like sparks from a fire, drifting upward, dissolving into the heavy sky. Tears that rise toward heaven instead of falling to earth.

He stands frozen, watching. The tears keep rising, a slow stream of grief returning to wherever grief comes from.

"Who are you mourning?" he asks.

She goes still. The sobbing stops. The silence that follows is absolute, not just quiet, but the complete absence of sound. The wind that was stirring the grass has stopped. The birds that were calling in the distance have gone silent. Even his own heartbeat seems to pause.

She turns.

Her face is familiar in a way he can't place, neither young nor old, neither beautiful nor plain. A face that could belong to anyone. To everyone.

But her eyes.

Her eyes hold a grief so vast it makes his own losses feel like shadows. A grief not for one death, but for all death. Not for one dismissal, but for every time someone saw the truth and was told they were wrong.

"Why are you weeping?" she asks.

The question catches him off guard. He wasn't weeping. He was asking about her grief, not his own.

But when he touches his face, his fingers come away wet.

"I don't..." he starts.

"Who are you looking for?" she asks. The same words, the ancient words, but now they're directed at him. "Who do you seek among the tombs?"

"I don't know," he whispers. "I don't know what I'm looking for anymore."

She rises. Stands before him. Her tears continue to lift from her face, rising like prayers.

"They didn't believe her," she says. "The first one to see. The one who went to tell them. They didn't believe her."

Mary. She's talking about Mary.

"They never believe the ones who see first," she continues. "The ones who run to share what they've witnessed. The ones whose hearts are still burning with what they've seen." She shakes her head slowly. "They dismiss. They doubt. They look for other explanations. Easier explanations."

Maybe there's something medical. A tumor.

"But she told anyway," the woman says. "She told because it was true. Not because they would believe. Not because they would accept. She told because she had seen, and seeing requires telling, and telling requires courage, even when no one believes."

He's weeping openly now. He doesn't know when he started. The tears fall down his face, not upward like hers, just ordinary human tears, falling the way tears are supposed to fall.

"How do you bear it?" he asks. "Being dismissed. Being doubted. Knowing what you know and having no one believe you."

She reaches out. Touches his face. Her hand is warm, unnaturally warm, and where she touches him, the grief shifts, not disappearing, but becoming something else. Something bearable.

"You bear it because the truth doesn't require belief to be true," she says. "You bear it because your commission is to tell, not to convince. You bear it because the one who sent you also bore it, was dismissed, was doubted, was rejected, and bore it anyway, and bears it still."

Her face begins to change. The features sharpening. The eyes becoming specific.

"Tell them," she says. "Even when they don't believe. Even when they call you sick. Even when the ones who love you look at you with fear. Tell them anyway. Tell them because it's true."

The face...

He gasps awake.

The bedroom is dark. Beth breathes beside him. The clock reads 3:47.

His face is wet. His chest aches with a grief that isn't his, or is his, now, transferred, shared. The grief of everyone who ever saw something true and was told they were wrong.

He lies still, staring at the ceiling. The dream clings to him like fog.

Tell them anyway. Tell them because it's true.

His eyes grow heavy. Sleep pulls at him again.

He doesn't resist.

A room.

Different from the cemetery. Completely different. He's indoors now, a small space, close and warm. A kitchen, maybe. Or a den. Somewhere arguments happen. Somewhere truth gets cornered.

He looks for a door.

There isn't one.

Four walls, solid and seamless. A table in the center, two chairs facing each other. A single lamp hanging overhead, casting a circle of yellow light. Beyond the light, shadows.

He's in one of the chairs. He doesn't remember sitting down.

The other chair is occupied.

A man. Middle-aged. Ordinary looking, the kind of face you'd pass on the street without noticing. He's leaning back, arms crossed, watching Lem with eyes that miss nothing.

"You've been having quite a time of it," the man says.

Lem doesn't answer. The woman in the cemetery, her grief was open, shared, almost gentle despite its weight. This man is something else. Something harder.

"Dreams. Visions. Voices." The man tilts his head. "And now you think you know something. Think you've been chosen for something."

"Who are you," Lem asks.

The man smiles. It's not a kind smile.

"You know who I am. You've been running from me your whole life." He leans forward. "I'm the question you don't want to answer. The truth you don't want to face. I'm everything you've hidden from yourself and everyone else."

The light flickers.

"That's not..."

"Don't." The man holds up a hand. "Don't lie. Not here. Not to me."

The light dims slightly. Lem feels it, a connection between his words and the illumination. The room responding to something.

"Every time you lie, it gets darker," the man says. "Every time you deflect, you lose a little more light. That's how this works. That's the only rule."

Lem grips the arms of the chair. "What do you want?"

"The same thing I always want. The same thing everyone who's ever loved you wants." The man's face flickers, for a split second, it's Lem's father. Then Bud. Then Father John. Then a stranger. Then something else entirely. "I want you to see yourself clearly. I want you to stop hiding."

"I'm not hiding."

The light dims.

"I said don't lie."

Lem's heart is pounding. The room feels smaller, the walls closer. The shadows at the edge of the light are thickening.

"You've been given words," the man says. "Teachings. Visions that would break most people. But do you know where they come from?"

"I know where they come from."

"Do you?" The man's eyes bore into him. "Do you know who else heard them? Do you know who was silenced? Do you know why you've never read these words before, why you had to discover them in dreams instead of in churches?"

Lem says nothing.

"Do you know who you're being asked to stand with? Mary, who was dismissed. Thomas, who was mocked for his doubt. Philip, who wrote in riddles because plain speech would have gotten him killed." The man leans closer. "Do you understand what it costs to join that company?"

"I understand."

"You understand *nothing*." The man's voice sharpens. "You think because you've had some dreams, because you've felt some presence, because you've heard some words, you think that makes you ready? You haven't even begun to face what's inside you."

"What's inside me?"

The man's face flickers again. Father. Friend. Priest. And beneath them all, something ancient, something that has been asking hard questions since the beginning of time.

"Fear," the man says. "You're afraid of what this will cost you. Your wife already looks at you like you're broken. Your daughter is questioning your sanity. Your priest sent you to a psychiatrist. And it will get worse. Much worse. Are you afraid?"

Lem's throat tightens. The light flickers.

"Yes," he whispers. "I'm afraid."

The light steadies. Grows slightly brighter.

"Good," the man says. "Fear is honest. Fear can be faced." He pauses. "What else?"

"What else what," Lem asks.

"What else is inside you? What else have you been hiding, from Beth, from Kate, from yourself?"

The room feels like a furnace now. The man's gaze is relentless.

"I don't know if I'm strong enough," Lem says. The words come out before he can stop them. "I don't know if I can do what's being asked. I don't know if I'm the right person. I keep waiting for someone more qualified to show up. Someone who knows the Bible better, who prays more, who hasn't spent his whole life just... drifting."

The light brightens.

"What else?"

"I'm angry." The admission surprises him. "At Father John, for not believing me. At Beth, for looking at me like I'm sick. At Kate, for wavering. I know they're afraid, I know they love me, but I'm still angry. And I feel guilty for being angry. And I feel alone."

The light is stronger now. The shadows retreating.

"What else?"

"I don't know if any of this is real." The deepest fear, finally spoken. "I don't know if I'm actually being visited, or if I'm just... losing my mind. Seeing what I want to see. Making meaning out of nothing."

He's shaking. The room is bright now, brighter than it was when the dream began. The man watches him with something that might be compassion, might be satisfaction, might be both.

"Seek and do not stop seeking until you find," the man says. His voice has changed, softer now, but with an edge that won't release. "When you find, you will be troubled. You are troubled, aren't you?"

"Yes."

"Good. That's how it's supposed to feel. The trouble comes before the marvel. The darkness comes before the light. You cannot skip to the end." The man stands. "You've been given words. Now find out where they come from. Find out who else heard them. Find out who was silenced and why."

"How?"

The man smiles. This time, the smile is almost kind.

"You know how. You've just been afraid to look."

He leans forward. The light blazes. His face begins to clarify, the features becoming specific, unmistakable, the face from every dream, the face Lem has been seeing in pieces since this all began...

He wakes.

The bedroom. Dark. Beth breathing. The clock reads 4:33.

Two hours since the cemetery. Two dreams in one night.

Lem lies still, his mind racing. The man's words echo: *Find out where they come from. Find out who was silenced.*

The words from the dreams. The teachings. He's assumed they were original, private revelations, personal messages. But the man spoke as if they existed somewhere else. As if they'd been heard before, written down, buried.

Do you know who else heard them?

He gets out of bed quietly, careful not to wake Beth. Walks to his office. Opens his laptop.

The screen glows in the darkness.

His fingers hover over the keyboard.

The kingdom of the Father is spread out upon the earth, and people do not see it.

He types the words into the search engine.

And presses enter.

Chapter Fifteen

The Discovery

The search results load.

Lem stares at the screen. The office is dark around him, the only light the glow of the laptop. Outside the window, the first gray hint of dawn touches the horizon.

The kingdom of the Father is spread out upon the earth, and people do not see it.

The words he typed. The words the fisherman spoke in the first dream, standing on his boat in the half-light of morning.

The first result: *Gospel of Thomas, Saying 113.*

He clicks.

A page of text. Scholarly, dense. He scans it, his heart beating faster.

The Gospel of Thomas is a non-canonical sayings gospel. It was discovered in 1945 near Nag Hammadi, Egypt, as part of a collection of thirteen ancient books (codices) containing over fifty texts. The manuscripts date to around 340 CE, though the original composition is believed to be much earlier, possibly as early as the first century.

Discovered in 1945. Buried in the Egyptian desert. Hidden in a clay jar for sixteen hundred years.

He scrolls.

The Gospel of Thomas consists of 114 sayings attributed to Jesus, many of which have parallels in the canonical gospels, but many of which are unique. Unlike Matthew, Mark, Luke, and John, Thomas contains no narrative, no birth story, no miracles, no crucifixion, no resurrection. Only sayings. Only words.

Only words.

Lem's hands are trembling. He didn't imagine this. He didn't make it up. The words from his dreams, they exist. They've existed for two thousand years.

Split a piece of wood; I am there. Lift a stone, and you will find me.

Gospel of Thomas, Saying 77.

The old man on the fish house dock, mending his net with gnarled fingers. *You keep looking for me in high places. But I'm here. Split a piece of driftwood. Lift a shell from the sand. I am there.*

He searches again:

If you bring forth what is within you, what you bring forth will save you.

Gospel of Thomas, Saying 70.

The waitress at Mike's. Darlene. Her tired eyes, her knowing smile. *Bring forth what is inside you. It's the only thing that saves.*

He searches again:

Seek and do not stop seeking until you find. When you find, you will be troubled.

Gospel of Thomas, Saying 2.

The challenger in the doorless room. *When you find, you will be troubled. You are troubled, aren't you?*

Every word. Every teaching. Every phrase that had felt like private revelation, they were all here. Written down. Preserved. Buried.

And then found.

He reads for hours.

The sky lightens outside his window. The marsh emerges from darkness. The water turns from black to gray to silver. He doesn't notice.

He's falling down a well of ancient text, a hidden history he never knew existed.

He learns about Nag Hammadi. A farmer digging for fertilizer near cliffs in Upper Egypt. A sealed clay jar. Fifty-two texts in thirteen leather-bound codices. The farmer's mother burning some of the pages for kindling before anyone realized what they were.

He learns about the other gospels. Not just Thomas, there were more. The Gospel of Philip. The Gospel of Mary. The Gospel of Truth. The Apocryphon of John. Texts attributed to disciples whose voices he'd never heard in church. Witnesses who had been silenced.

Do you know who was silenced?

He searches: *Gospel of Mary.*

A different text. Fragments, mostly, the beginning and middle are lost, only pieces remain. But what remains is enough.

Mary Magdalene. Not the prostitute the church made her, that was a lie, a conflation. Mary the disciple. Mary the apostle. Mary who saw the risen Christ first, before any of the men. Mary who went to tell them what she'd seen.

And they didn't believe her.

He reads the text. Peter, angry, dismissive: *Did he really speak with a woman without our knowledge? Are we to turn and listen to her? Did he prefer her to us?*

And Levi, Matthew, defending her: *If the Savior made her worthy, who are you to reject her? Surely the Savior knows her very well. That is why he loved her more than us.*

If the Savior made her worthy, who are you to reject her?

Lem stops. Rereads the line.

Bud's voice on the boat, just yesterday: *If God made you worthy of this, whatever this is... I'm not going to be the one to reject it.*

The same words. The same defense. Two thousand years apart.

Bud didn't know. Couldn't have known. He'd never read the Gospel of Mary, probably never heard of it. But the words came through him anyway, the ancient voice of Levi speaking through a fisherman in North Carolina, defending a witness against the ones who doubted.

Lem's eyes are wet. He wipes his face with the back of his hand.

He searches: *Gospel of Philip.*

Another voice. Another witness. Philip, writing about truth and images, about names and their deceptions, about mysteries that could only be spoken in symbol and metaphor.

Truth did not come into the world naked, but it came in types and images. The world will not receive truth in any other way.

The woman in the gallery. The painting that shifted. *The images are how I come to those I love. The fisherman. The child. The waitress in the diner. These are not masks. They are kindness.*

Philip knew. Two thousand years ago, Philip understood what Lem is only now beginning to grasp, that truth wears forms because raw truth would destroy. That the disguises are not deception but mercy.

He keeps reading.

He learns about the Council of Nicaea. 325 CE. Constantine, the Roman emperor who converted to Christianity and then shaped it to serve empire. The beginning of a process that would eventually decide which books would be Scripture and which would be heresy. Which voices would be heard and which would be silenced.

Thomas, Mary, Philip, they lost. Their gospels were declared heretical. Their words were banned. Their books were burned wherever they were found.

But someone hid them. Someone sealed them in a jar and buried them in the Egyptian cliffs and trusted that someday, somehow, they would be found again.

Sixteen hundred years later, a farmer's shovel struck clay.

Lem sits back in his chair.

The sun is fully up now, the office bright with morning light. He can hear Beth moving in the kitchen, the sounds of coffee being made. Duke's nails clicking on the hardwood floor.

He looks at the screen. Tabs open, Thomas, Mary, Philip, Nag Hammadi, early Christianity, gnostic texts, the formation of the canon. A hidden world, a buried history, a conversation that was silenced before it could be heard.

Do you know who else heard them?

Now he knows.

Do you know who was silenced?

Now he knows.

Do you know why you've never read these words before, why you had to discover them in dreams instead of in churches?

Now he knows.

The church made a choice. Sixteen centuries ago, men in power decided which witnesses would speak and which would be silent. They chose Peter over Mary. They chose the resurrection narrative over the inner kingdom. They chose the institution over the individual encounter.

And the other voices, the ones who said the kingdom was here, now, spread out upon the earth if only you could see it; the ones who said the truth was inside you, waiting to be brought forth; the ones who said you didn't need a priest or a temple or an institution because Christ was in the split wood and the lifted stone, those voices were buried.

Until now.

Mary told. Thomas went.

The words from... where? A dream he hasn't had yet? A teaching he hasn't received? He doesn't know. But he feels them, pressing against the inside of his chest, waiting to be understood.

Mary told. Even though they didn't believe her. Even though Peter dismissed her. She told because she had seen, and seeing requires telling.

Thomas went. Doubted and then believed. Touched the wounds and knew. Traveled east, according to tradition, all the way to India, carrying the teaching, planting seeds that would grow for centuries.

Mary told. Thomas went.

And someone buried their words in a jar, trusting that the silence wouldn't last forever.

Lem closes the laptop.

He sits in the growing light, surrounded by the ordinary objects of his ordinary life, the bookshelf, the desk, the window looking out on the water. Everything looks the same.

Everything is different.

He's not crazy. He's not having a breakdown. The words he's been hearing are real, ancient, true. They were spoken two thousand years ago and they're still being spoken now, breaking through in dreams and visions and moments of unexpected grace.

Bring forth what is inside you.

He knows now what's inside him. The same thing that was inside Mary, inside Thomas, inside Philip. The same witness. The same commission. The same impossible task: to tell the truth even when no one believes, to carry the teaching even when the institution has declared it heresy, to trust that someday, somehow, the silence will be broken.

He stands.

Beth is calling from the kitchen. Breakfast. Coffee. The normal rhythms of a normal Saturday.

He walks out of the office. Down the hall. Into the kitchen where his wife is waiting.

He doesn't tell her yet. Not yet. The discovery is too new, too raw, too overwhelming. He needs to sit with it. To let it settle. To understand what it means before he tries to explain it to someone else.

But he will tell her. Eventually. He'll tell all of them.

Because that's what witnesses do.

They tell.

Chapter Sixteen

The Temple

He doesn't know how he got here.

One moment he was in bed, Beth beside him, the house dark, the familiar weight of Saturday pressing toward Sunday, and now he's here. Sitting in a seat he doesn't remember choosing, surrounded by thousands of people he doesn't know.

A mega-church. The kind he's seen on television, the kind that fills stadiums, the kind with screens the size of billboards and lighting rigs that could illuminate a concert. The seats stretch up and away in every direction, a vast bowl of humanity, and every seat is filled.

The seat beside him is empty.

Then it isn't.

A man settles in next to him. Middle-aged. Dark hair, olive skin, ordinary clothes, jeans, a plain button-down shirt, nothing that would draw attention. He glances at Lem the way strangers do in public spaces. A small nod. Acknowledgment. Nothing more.

Lem nods back.

The lights dim. The crowd hushes. A worship band takes the stage, guitars, drums, keyboards, backup singers in matching outfits. The music begins.

It's huge. Overwhelming. The bass thrums in Lem's chest. The screens display lyrics in massive white letters. Fog machines fill the stage with haze. Colored lights sweep across the crowd.

The people rise. Thousands of them, all at once, hands lifting toward the ceiling. The sound of their voices joins the music, a wall of praise, a tsunami of worship.

The man beside Lem stands too.

Lem watches him.

The man isn't looking at the stage. He's looking at the people. His face is turned slightly, taking in the rows and rows of lifted hands, the swaying bodies, the closed eyes and open mouths.

And his expression...

Lem's breath catches.

The man's eyes are bright. Almost wet. There's something on his face that Lem can only call *tenderness*. A love so vast it seems to fill the space between them, spilling over, touching everyone in the room.

He loves them, Lem thinks. *He actually loves them. All of them.*

The worship continues. The man closes his eyes. His lips move slightly, prayer or song, Lem can't tell. The music builds and crests and builds again.

Lem feels something he hasn't felt in weeks. Peace. Safety. A sense that whatever is happening, whatever is coming, he is not alone.

The music fades. The crowd sits. The screens shift to a logo, the church's name in sleek, modern letters. A countdown appears: the sermon is about to begin.

The preacher takes the stage.

He's in his fifties, maybe sixty. Silver hair, perfect teeth, an expensive suit that fits like it was sewn onto his body. He moves with the easy confidence of a man who has stood on this stage a thousand times, who knows exactly how the light hits his face, exactly when to pause for applause.

"Welcome, church!" His voice booms through the sound system. "Welcome *home*!"

The crowd erupts. Applause, cheers, scattered amens.

The man beside Lem claps too. Gently. His face still holds that tenderness.

"God is good, isn't He?" the preacher says. "And He wants *good things* for you."

The crowd responds. The preacher grins, basking in it.

Lem glances at the man beside him.

His hands have gone still. They rest on his knees now, motionless.

The sermon begins. The screens display graphics, slick, professional. Words appear in bold letters: SUCCESS. BLESSING. VICTORY.

"God doesn't want you to struggle," the preacher says. "He wants you to *thrive*. He wants you to *win*. He has plans for your prosperity, plans to give you a future and hope."

The crowd applauds.

The man's fingers curl slightly. Just slightly. A tension that wasn't there before.

The preacher's tone shifts. His voice drops, becomes conspiratorial, intimate despite the thousands listening.

"But there are those who want to take that from you. There are *enemies* of everything we hold dear."

The screens change. Images flash, news footage, protests, faces that are clearly meant to represent *the other*. The people who don't belong. The threats.

"They want to take what is ours. They want to erase our faith. They call themselves Christians, but are they *really*?"

The crowd murmurs agreement. Some people shake their heads. Some call out.

The man beside Lem is no longer smiling.

His jaw has tightened. His breathing has changed, slower, deeper, the breath of someone controlling themselves.

The preacher builds momentum. His voice rises.

"This is *our* country. *Our* faith. *Our* values. And we will *not* apologize!"

Wild applause. People on their feet. The noise is deafening.

The man does not stand.

Lem looks at him, really looks.

And what he sees stops his heart.

The man's eyes are fixed on the preacher. Fixed and burning. Not with hatred, with something older, deeper, more terrible. A grief so profound it has become fire. A love so fierce it has become judgment.

Lem has seen those eyes before. On the boat. On the beach. At the fish house dock. At Mike's, in the gallery, in the cemetery.

He knows those eyes.

The preacher reaches his crescendo. His arms spread wide, his face lifted to the lights.

"*Jesus* is on our side! He *always* has been! And with *Him*, we will take back what is *ours*! We will make America great again!"

The crowd erupts.

The man stands.

But not to applaud.

He stands the way someone stands when they have seen enough. When patience has reached its end. When silence is no longer possible.

The lights flicker.

The screens glitch, loss of signal for a split second, then back. The crowd murmurs. The preacher hesitates, glances offstage.

The man speaks.

He doesn't shout. His voice isn't loud. But it cuts through everything, the music, the murmurs, the massive sound system. It fills the room the way light fills a space, the way water fills a vessel. It is simply *there*, everywhere at once.

"You have taken my name."

The preacher stops. Looks around, confused.

"You have taken my name and made it a sword against the very ones I came to save."

The lights flicker again. Longer this time. The screens flash with static.

People look around, unsettled. Some pull out their phones. Some whisper to each other.

The man continues. His voice is steady, measured, heavy with a sorrow that seems to press down on the air itself.

"You lock the doors of the kingdom and stand guard. You choose not to enter yourselves. And those who are trying to enter, you stop them."

The preacher taps his microphone. "We're having some technical difficulties..."

"I was hungry."

The screens flicker. The preacher's graphics disappear. New images take their place. Faces. Thin faces. Children with hollow eyes. Refugees at borders. The homeless on street corners.

"I was a stranger."

More faces. People turned away. People detained. People told they don't belong.

"I was sick. I was imprisoned."

Arrests. Detention centers. The images keep coming, flooding every screen in the auditorium, unstoppable.

The crowd is murmuring now. Fear is setting in. Some are standing, looking for exits. Some are frozen in their seats, staring at the screens with something like horror.

The preacher has backed away from the podium. His face is pale.

The man turns slightly, just enough that Lem can see him fully.

His eyes.

Not rage. Not fury.

Grief. Bottomless grief. The sorrow of a father watching his children destroy each other in his name. The heartbreak of a love that has been twisted into a weapon.

"You have made my Father's house a marketplace," the man says. "You have sold what was never yours to sell."

He looks at the preacher. Directly. The preacher cannot hold his gaze. He stumbles backward, nearly falls.

"I drove out the money changers once."

A pause. The silence is immense. Even the murmuring has stopped. Thousands of people holding their breath.

"Do you think I have forgotten how?"

Every light in the auditorium goes dark.

Screams. Confusion. The sound of thousands of people in sudden darkness, stumbling, crying out, reaching for each other.

Lem doesn't move. He sits frozen in his seat, his heart pounding, his eyes adjusting to the darkness.

Emergency lights flicker on, red, dim, barely enough to see. The exit signs glow like distant fires.

In the red half-light, the man turns to Lem.

Their eyes meet.

The grief is still there. But something else too. Tenderness. Specifically for him. The same look Lem saw in the gallery, in the cemetery, in every dream. The look that says: *You are not the target. You are the witness. You are being prepared.*

The man opens his mouth to speak...

* * *

Lem wakes gasping.

The bedroom. The clock reads 3:47. The sound of waves through the window. Beth stirring beside him.

He sits up. His face is wet, tears or sweat, he can't tell. His hands are shaking.

He looks toward the window. The shore. The water. The ordinary world going about its ordinary business.

But nothing is ordinary anymore.

He has seen it now. The Christ of the fishing boat and the Christ of the temple. The tenderness and the fury. The love that holds and the love that overturns tables.

They are the same.

They have always been the same.

He lies back down. Beth murmurs something, reaches for him in her sleep. He takes her hand. Holds it.

The dreams have been leading somewhere. He understands that now. Each one a step, a preparation, a piece of something larger.

The fishing boat taught him to see.

The child taught him humility.

The old fisherman taught him presence.

The waitress and the homeless man taught him compassion.

The gallery taught him why truth wears forms.

The cemetery taught him to tell anyway.

The challenger taught him to face himself.

And the temple...

The temple taught him that love has teeth. That mercy has limits. That the same hands that break bread can braid a whip.

He closes his eyes.

One more dream. He can feel it waiting for him. One more step before whatever comes next.

He's ready.

Chapter Seventeen

Shackleford

Sunday morning.

Lem wakes before dawn. The house is dark. Beth is still sleeping, her breathing slow and even, her hand curled on the pillow where his head was.

He lies still for a moment, watching her. Thirty years. The curve of her cheek. The gray in her hair that she stopped dyeing last year. The woman who has stood beside him through everything, the lean years, the good years, the years when the writing came easy and the years when it wouldn't come at all.

She's afraid for him. He knows that. Afraid of what's happening, afraid of what it means, afraid she's losing him to something she can't see or touch or understand.

He wishes he could explain it to her. Wishes he had words that would make sense of the dreams, the visitors, the ancient teachings that have been pouring into him like water into a vessel. But some things can't be explained. Some things can only be lived.

He slips out of bed. Dresses quietly. Jeans, a flannel shirt, his old fishing jacket. The clothes of a man going to the water.

Duke raises his head from his bed in the corner, tail thumping once.

"Stay, boy," Lem whispers. "I'll be back."

The dog lowers his head.

* * *

He moves through the house in the gray half-light. Kitchen. Living room. The familiar shapes of furniture, the photographs on the walls, the accumulation of a life.

He stops at the hall closet. Pulls out the camping gear he hasn't used in years, the small tent, the sleeping bag, the cookstove. He packs them into a duffel, along with water, food, a flashlight, matches.

He's not sure how long he'll be gone. A day. Maybe two. However long it takes.

He writes a note. Leaves it on the kitchen counter where Beth will find it:

Gone to Shackleford. I have to do this. I'll be back. I love you. - Lem
It's not enough. He knows it's not enough. But it's all he has.

* * *

The dock is silver in the early light.

He walks down the weathered boards, the duffel over his shoulder, his footsteps soft in the stillness. The Pathfinder rocks gently in its slip at the end, waiting for him the way it's waited a thousand mornings before.

He loads the gear. Checks the fuel. Runs through the pre-departure routine he's done so many times before.

The engine catches. The water burbles at the stern. He casts off the lines, backs out of the slip, threads through the channel.

The sun breaks the horizon as he clears the shallows.

He opens the throttle.

* * *

The Banks rise out of the water like a dream.

Shackleford. Nine miles of sand and dune and maritime forest, curved like a crescent moon along the edge of the Atlantic. No bridges. No roads. No permanent structures. Just the island, the wild horses, and the endless sky.

Lem has been coming here since those first college summers. Bud brought him, taught him to anchor in the shallows on the sound side, to wade ashore with the cooler, to respect the horses and give them space. Later, he brought Beth. Later still, Kate. The island holds their history like the rings of a tree.

But he's never come alone like this. Never come with this weight in his chest, this certainty that something is waiting for him.

He approaches, finds his spot, a shallow cove protected from the wind, sandy bottom, good holding. He cuts the engine. Drops the anchor. Feels it set.

The silence is immense.

No traffic. No voices. No hum of electricity. Just the lap of water against the hull, the cry of gulls, the whisper of wind through the sea oats on the dunes.

He sits for a moment, letting it settle over him. The peace of it. The emptiness that isn't empty at all.

Then he gathers his gear, slips over the side into the knee-deep water, and wades ashore.

* * *

The crossing takes nearly an hour.

He walks through the maritime forest, twisted live oaks draped with Spanish moss, wax myrtles, red cedars bent by decades of salt wind. The trail is narrow, sandy, barely visible in places. He's walked it before, but not recently. Not in quite a while.

The horses watch him pass. A small band of them, a stallion, three mares, and a foal. They stand among the trees like ghosts, their dark eyes tracking his movement. They don't spook. They've seen humans before. They simply watch, and wait, and let him go.

He emerges from the forest onto the dunes.

And there it is.

The Atlantic.

It stretches to the horizon, vast and gray-green, the waves rolling in with a rhythm as old as time. The beach is empty, miles of sand in both directions, not a single footprint, not a single sign of human presence.

He stands at the top of the dune and breathes.

This is where he's supposed to be. He doesn't know how he knows it, but he knows it. Every dream, every visitor, every word spoken in the night, they've all been leading here. To this beach. To this moment.

To whatever comes next.

* * *

He makes camp above the tide line, up near the dunes.

The tent goes up easy, muscle memory, the body remembering what the mind has forgotten. He gathers driftwood. Builds a fire ring with sand. Lays out his sleeping bag.

The afternoon passes slowly. He walks the beach, looking for nothing, finding everything. Shells tumbled smooth by the surf. A pelican diving for fish. The tracks of ghost crabs in the wet sand, disappearing into tiny holes.

Split a piece of wood; I am there. Lift a shell, and you will find me.

He picks up a piece of driftwood. Gray and weathered, salt-cured, smooth as bone. He turns it over in his hands.

Is he here? In this?

He sets it down. Keeps walking.

* * *

The sun sinks toward the mainland.

Lem sits by the unlit fire, watching the colors change, gold to orange to pink to purple. The water darkens. The first stars emerge, faint at first, then brighter as the sky deepens.

He thinks about what he's learned. The hours at his laptop, falling down the well of ancient texts. Thomas, who walked with Christ and doubted and believed and carried the teaching all the way to India. Mary, who saw first and was dismissed and told anyway. Philip, who understood that truth comes in types and images because the world cannot receive it any other way.

Their words buried for sixteen centuries. Their voices silenced by men who feared what they had to say. And then a farmer's shovel striking clay, and the silence finally breaking.

He thinks about Bud. Out on the water in the old Sea Ox, listening without judgment, and then saying the words that echoed across two thousand years: *If God made you worthy of this, whatever this is... I'm not going to be the one to reject it.* Levi defending Mary. Bud defending Lem. The chain unbroken.

He thinks about Father John. The trembling hand at the communion rail. The flicker of recognition in his eyes. And then the careful retreat, the institutional caution, the recommendation for a psychiatrist. A man who felt the truth and turned away. Lem doesn't hate him for it. Fear is human. But it still cuts.

He thinks about Kate. Sweet Kate. Who sat across from him on the boat and said *I believe YOU*, and meant it, in that moment, with her whole heart. And then wavered. And then talked to her mother about tumors and treatments. He doesn't blame her either. She loves him. Love makes people afraid.

And Beth. The love of his life. Thirty years of marriage, thirty years of building something together, and now she looks at him like he's a stranger. Like something has taken her husband and left this other person in his place. She's not wrong. Something has taken him. But it hasn't replaced him, it's *revealed* him. The Lem who was always there, underneath, waiting to be called.

He lights the fire. The driftwood catches slowly, then blazes. The flames push back the darkness, create a circle of warmth and light.

He eats a little. Drinks some water. Watches the fire burn down to coals.

The stars wheel overhead. The Milky Way emerges, a river of light across the black sky, more stars than he's seen in years. The island has no light pollution. The darkness here is real darkness, and the light is real light.

He thinks about the dreams. All of them. The fisherman on the boat. The child on the shore. The old man with the net. The waitress and the homeless man. The woman in the gallery. The weeping woman in the cemetery. The challenger in the doorless room. The temple, the preacher, the grief that became fire.

Nine encounters. Nine pieces of something he's only beginning to understand.

And now he's here. On the island. Waiting for the tenth.

He doesn't know what form it will take. Doesn't know what words will be spoken, if any words are spoken at all. But he knows it's coming. He can feel it the way you feel a storm building on the horizon, the pressure changing, the air going electric.

Something is coming.

He's ready.

* * *

The fire dies to embers. The cold creeps in.

Lem wraps himself in the sleeping bag but doesn't go into the tent. He wants to see the sky. Wants to be awake when it happens.

The beach is dark. The waves are a rhythm without a shape, heard but not seen. The stars burn cold and distant overhead.

He lies there, waiting.

And that's when it begins.

Not a voice. Not at first. Just a feeling, a weight settling on his chest, a tightening in his throat. The way the air felt in the doorless room, in the dream where he was challenged, accused, forced to defend what he knew.

But this isn't a dream. He's awake. Eyes open. Stars overhead.

And the whisper comes.

What are you doing here?

It sounds like his own thought. His own voice, the reasonable part of him that has been quiet these past weeks but never quite gone.

What are you doing on this beach, in the cold, alone? Waiting for what?

He doesn't answer. Just lies there, watching the stars.

Beth is at home. Afraid. Because of you.

The words land somewhere deep. Because they're true. Beth *is* afraid. He saw it in her eyes before he left. The fear she tries to hide. The way she looks at him now, searching for the man she married, finding someone she doesn't recognize.

She's lying awake right now. Wondering if you're okay. Wondering if you're coming back. Wondering if she's losing you.

Lem closes his eyes. The weight on his chest grows heavier.

And Kate. Your Katie. She believed you on the boat, remember that? She looked you in the eye and said she believed you. And now she's running differentials in her head. Temporal lobe. Tumor. Something treatable.

They think you're broken, Lem.

He feels the sting of it. The truth wrapped in poison.

Father John thinks so too. That's why he sent you to a psychiatrist.

The whisper pauses. The waves roll in, roll out. The stars are cold.

What if they're right?

Lem's eyes are open.

What if you've imagined all of it? The dreams, the visitors, the words you can't get out of your head? What if there's no one coming to this beach tomorrow? What if you sit here all night and nothing happens, and you have to go home and tell Beth it was nothing, and watch the relief in her eyes, and know that the relief is because she thinks you're finally getting better?

The doubt is heavy. So heavy. Because he can't prove anything. Can't point to evidence. Can't offer anything but his own experience, and experience can be wrong. Minds can break. Men can lose themselves in dreams and never find their way back.

You're a fisherman, Lem. A writer. You're not a prophet. You're not special. You're just a man who stopped sleeping and started having vivid dreams, and somewhere along the way you convinced yourself they meant something.

The weight presses down. The cold seeps in.

Go home. Now. Before dawn. Slip back into bed beside Beth and hold her and tell her you're sorry. Tell her you got confused. Tell her you're going to see the doctor, get the tests, find out what's wrong. Be a good husband. Be a good father. Be normal.

You can still be normal, Lem. It's not too late.

He lies in the darkness, the whisper coiling around him like a snake.

And he recognizes it.

Not the voice, the voice sounds like him, sounds reasonable, sounds like concern and wisdom. But beneath the voice, beneath the reasonable words, there's something else. A pressure. A pushing. Something that wants him to quit. To leave. To give up and go home.

He's felt this before. Not in the dreams, in life. In the moments when he was about to do something that mattered. The fear before he asked Beth to marry him. The doubt before he sent out his first manuscript. The whisper that said *who do you think you are?* every time he stepped toward something larger than himself.

He knows this voice.

It's not him. It is the whisper of the enemy.

And in that knowing, something else rises. Not argument. Not rebuke. Just the thing he's always done, the reflex of a lifetime.

He prays.

Not formally. Not with eloquence. Just the way he's prayed over a thousand fish pulled from the water, over a thousand meals, in a thousand quiet moments when no one was listening.

Thank you for Beth.

The whisper doesn't respond. As if it has no words for this.

Thank you for Kate.

He says it aloud now, soft in the darkness. Just a murmur. Just a man praying on a beach.

"Thank you for this life."

The weight on his chest doesn't vanish. But the whisper, the whisper has stopped. Not argued away. Not defeated. Just... silent. As if it opened its mouth and found nothing to say. As if gratitude were a language it didn't speak.

Lem lies still. The waves roll in, roll out. The fire has faded to ash.

He waits for the whisper to return. Waits for the pressure, the doubt, the reasonable voice telling him to go home.

It doesn't come.

The cold is still there. The dark is still there. But something has shifted. The darkness isn't pressing anymore. It's just night. Just the ordinary dark of a beach under stars. The weight is gone.

He looks up at the sky. The same stars. The same Milky Way. But they seem closer now. Warmer. As if the universe has softened around him.

He doesn't understand what happened. Doesn't feel like he won anything. He just prayed. The way he's always prayed. And the whisper took leave from him.

His eyes grow heavy. The exhaustion settles in, bone deep, the tiredness of a man who has carried too much for too long.

He doesn't fight it.

The stars wheel slowly overhead. The waves keep their rhythm. The fire is ash and ember, a faint glow in the darkness.

But it's not as dark as it was.

He sleeps.

* * *

Beth wakes to an empty bed.

Her hand finds his pillow before her eyes open, the old habit, reaching for him in the half-light. But the pillow is cold. The sheets on his side undisturbed.

She lies still for a moment, heart pounding.

She gets up. Pulls on her robe. Walks to the window.

The bay is silver in the early light. The dock stretches out, empty. The slip at the end where the Pathfinder should be holds only water.

She presses her hand against the glass. It's cold.

She finds the note. He's out there somewhere. On that island. Alone.

She should be angry. Should be furious that he left without waking her, without explaining, without giving her a chance to talk him out of it. But the anger won't come. There's only this, the emptiness of the house without him, the weight of not knowing, the fear she can't push away.

She thinks about church. It's Sunday. In two hours, the congregation will gather at St. Paul's. They'll sing the hymns. They'll speak the prayers. They'll kneel at the rail and receive the bread and wine.

And she won't be there.

She can't. Can't sit in that pew alone. Can't face the questions: *Where's Lem? Is everything okay?*, from people who mean well but don't understand. Can't pretend that this is a normal Sunday when nothing is normal anymore.

For the first time in thirty years, Beth Roberson will miss church.

The thought should bother her more than it does. The liturgy has been her anchor, her rhythm, the steady heartbeat of her faith. But today, the thought of sitting in that pew...*their* pew, third from the back, left side, without Lem beside her...

She can't.

Maybe she's been meeting God in the shallows while Lem has been pulled into the deep. Maybe her faith was always smaller than she thought, tidy, contained, comfortable. Maybe she never had to choose between the God she understood and the God who breaks all categories.

Until now.

She stays home. Makes coffee she doesn't drink. Stands at the window, watching the water, watching the empty slip where the Pathfinder should be.

And she prays.

Not the formal prayers of the liturgy. Not the words she's memorized over decades. Just the raw, ragged cry of a woman who doesn't know what else to do.

Please. Please bring him back to me. Please let him be okay. Please help me understand. Please...

She doesn't know how to finish. Doesn't know what she's asking for anymore.

Is she asking God to stop what's happening to Lem? To bring him back to normal? But what if normal isn't where he's supposed to be? What if this, all of this, is God's answer to thirty years of prayers she didn't even know she was praying?

She thinks of Father John's words. *The church is cautious about these things.* She'd felt relief when he said it. Finally, someone with authority was going to contain this, explain it, make it manageable. A psychiatrist. A diagnosis. Something with a name and a treatment plan.

But what if there is no diagnosis? What if Lem isn't sick?

What if he's the sanest he's ever been?

The morning passes. The light shifts on the water. The coffee grows cold.

Beth doesn't move.

* * *

She calls Kate at noon.

She doesn't plan to. Doesn't know what she's going to say until she hears her daughter's voice, brisk, professional, the voice of a woman between patients or meetings or whatever fills her days at Duke.

"Mom? Is everything okay?"

And Beth breaks.

The tears come without warning, great heaving sobs that shake her whole body. She can't speak. Can't explain. Can only cry into the phone while her daughter's voice sharpens with alarm.

"Mom. Mom, talk to me. What's wrong? Is it Dad?"

"He's gone," Beth manages. "He went to Shackleford, early this morning. He left a note."

Silence. Then: "Is he okay? Did something happen?"

"I don't know. He said he had to go. He said he'd be back." She's gasping now, trying to catch her breath. "I don't know what's happening, Katie. I don't know what to do."

"Okay." Kate's voice is calm. The physician's voice, the one that steadies patients and families in crisis. "Okay, Mom. Listen to me. I'm coming."

"You don't have to..."

"I'm coming. I'll be there tonight. Just... stay by the phone. If he calls, if anything changes, let me know. But I'm coming."

"Katie..."

"I love you, Mom. It's going to be okay. I don't know how, but it's going to be okay."

The line goes dead.

Beth sits there, the phone in her hand, tears still streaming down her face. But something has loosened in her chest. Kate is coming. She won't have to wait alone.

She wipes her face. Blows her nose. Gets up and pours out the cold coffee.

There's nothing to do now but wait.

* * *

Kate arrives a little after eight.

The headlights sweep across the front windows, and Beth is at the door before the engine cuts off. She watches her daughter climb out of the car, still in her work clothes, an overnight bag over her shoulder, her face tight with worry.

They meet on the porch. Beth pulls Kate into her arms and holds on.

She wants to ask the questions she always asks. *Are you eating? Are you sleeping? Is there anyone?* The questions that drive Kate crazy, the mother's hope that never quite dies. But not tonight. Tonight there's only this, her daughter in her arms, the two of them holding each other in the dark while somewhere out there, miles across the water, Lem sleeps on a beach and waits for God knows what.

"Any word?" Kate asks.

"Nothing. His phone is off. Or there's no signal."

Kate nods. She didn't expect anything different.

They go inside. Beth makes tea. Kate sits at the kitchen table, in the chair that's usually Lem's, and Beth feels a pang at that, her daughter in her husband's place, the wrong person in the right seat.

"Tell me everything," Kate says.

So Beth does. The empty bed. The note. The morning spent staring at the water. The church she couldn't attend. The prayers she couldn't finish.

Kate listens without interrupting. When Beth is done, she reaches across the table and takes her mother's hands.

"He's okay, Mom. I don't know how I know that, but I do. Whatever's happening to him, it's not going to hurt him."

"How can you be sure?"

"I can't. Not really." Kate's eyes are bright, but steady. "But I sat with him on that boat, and I listened to him describe what he's been experiencing. And I've seen psychosis, Mom. I've seen delusion. I've seen what happens when a mind breaks." She shakes her head slowly. "This isn't that. Dad isn't broken. He's... I don't know. Being called. Being opened. Something."

Beth looks at her daughter. The child she raised in that church, in that pew, with those hymns. The acolyte who carried the cross. The choir girl who sang the anthems. The woman who still goes, when she can, who hasn't left the faith even if she holds it differently now.

"Father John said he might be having a breakdown. Said we should rule out medical causes."

"Father John is scared." Kate's voice is gentle, but certain. "He felt something at that communion rail, I could see it in his face when you described it. He felt it, and he didn't know what to do with it. So he reached for the explanation that felt safest."

"Is that what I've been doing?"

Kate doesn't answer right away. She looks at her mother, really looks, the way she looks at patients when she's about to deliver hard news.

"I think we've all been doing that. You, me, Father John. Looking for a way to make this small enough to fit inside what we already understand." She squeezes Beth's hands. "But what if it's not small? What if Dad is exactly where he's supposed to be, doing exactly what he's supposed to do?"

Beth closes her eyes. The tears are coming again, she's cried more today than she has in years.

"I'm so scared, Katie."

"I know."

"I don't want to lose him."

"You're not going to lose him." Kate's voice is firm. "He said he'd come back. Dad doesn't lie. He's never lied, not once in your whole marriage. If he says he's coming back, he's coming back."

Beth nods. Wipes her face. Takes a breath.

"Will you stay? Until he comes home?"

"Of course. I'm not going anywhere."

They sit together in the kitchen, mother and daughter, as the night deepens around them. They don't talk much more. There's nothing more to say. But Kate's presence is enough, the steadiness of her, the faith she carries even when she doesn't know what to believe.

Beth thinks about the pew at St. Paul's. The one she couldn't face alone this morning. She thinks about all the Sundays she's sat there beside Lem, their hands touching during the prayers, their voices joining on the hymns. She's always thought of that as her faith, the showing up, the being present, the steady rhythm of a life lived in the pews.

But maybe faith is also this. Sitting in a kitchen at midnight, waiting for someone you love to come back from a place you can't follow. Trusting that God is still God, even when God works in ways you don't understand.

She reaches for her daughter's hand.

Kate takes it.

They wait.

Chapter Eighteen

The Light

He wakes in the dark.

Not suddenly, not gasping, not startled. Just a slow surfacing, like rising through deep water toward a surface he can't yet see.

The fire has gone cold. The stars still burn overhead, but they've wheeled westward, hours have passed. The Milky Way has shifted, the constellations rearranged themselves while he slept.

He lies still in his sleeping bag, listening.

The waves. The endless rhythm of them, rolling in and drawing back. The wind through the sea oats. The small sounds of the island at night, rustling, settling, breathing.

But there's something else.

A stillness beneath the sounds. A presence in the darkness.

He sits up.

The beach stretches before him, pale sand glowing faintly under starlight. The water is black, edged with phosphorescence where the waves break. The sky is immense, more sky than he's ever seen, the dome of it pressing down and lifting up at the same time.

And at the water's edge...

Light.

Not moonlight. The moon has set. Not starlight, this is something else. Something that doesn't come from the sky.

A figure. Standing at the tideline. But not a figure, not really. A shape. A presence. Made entirely of light.

No features. No face. No form he can name. Just radiance, soft and immense, standing where the waves touch the sand.

Lem's heart is pounding. He should be afraid. He isn't.

He pushes off the sleeping bag. Stands. His legs are unsteady beneath him, from sleep, from cold, from something else entirely.

He walks toward the water.

The sand is cool under his bare feet. When did he take off his boots? He doesn't remember. It doesn't matter. He walks, and the light waits for him, patient, still.

The waves roll in. The phosphorescence glitters. The light doesn't move.

He stops ten feet away. Close enough to feel it, a warmth on his face, on his chest, like standing near a fire. But there's no heat. Just... presence. A fullness in the air. A weight that isn't heavy.

He wants to speak. Wants to ask the questions that have been building in him for weeks: *Who are you? Why me? What do you want from me?*

But the words won't come. His throat is closed. His mouth won't open.

And he understands: this isn't a conversation. This isn't a teaching. This is something else.

This is preparation.

The light pulses. Slowly. Rhythmically. And Lem realizes, it's pulsing with his heartbeat. Or his heartbeat is pulsing with it. He can't tell which came first. They're synchronized, matched, two rhythms become one.

He looks up.

The stars are moving.

Not wheeling slowly the way they should, the patient rotation of the earth. They're *moving*, drifting, rearranging, clustering. He watches, breathless, as they gather themselves into a shape.

A cross? No, not quite. A fish? The ancient symbol, the secret sign of the early church? Maybe. Or maybe something older. Something he doesn't have a name for. A shape that means *recognition*. A shape that means *you know me*.

The tide stops.

He looks down. The waves have frozen mid-break, the foam suspended, the water held in place like glass. The phosphorescence hangs motionless, a thousand tiny lights caught in amber.

Time has stopped. Or he's stepped outside of it. He doesn't know which.

The light figure raises a hand.

Not reaching for him, just lifting. A gesture. A greeting. An acknowledgment.

And Lem feels it.

Heat on his face. Not burning, blessing. A warmth that goes deeper than skin, deeper than muscle, deeper than bone. It reaches into the place where he keeps his fear, his doubt, his unworthiness, and it touches those things, and it doesn't destroy them but it *sees* them, and the seeing is enough.

He is known.

Completely. Utterly. Every hidden thing, every shameful thing, every secret he's never told anyone, known. And not condemned. Not judged. Just known, and loved anyway.

Tears stream down his face. He doesn't feel them start. They're just there, falling, catching the light.

He wants to fall to his knees. Wants to prostrate himself on the sand, press his face to the earth, hide from the radiance that sees everything.

But he can't move. And he understands, he's not supposed to move. He's supposed to stand. To receive. To let himself be seen.

The light doesn't speak. No words come, not audibly, not in his mind, not in any way he can describe. But something is communicated. Something is transferred. A knowing that bypasses language entirely.

Tomorrow.

Not a word. A certainty. Planted in his chest like a seed.

Tomorrow, at dawn. Here. The real thing. Not a dream. Not a vision. The thing itself.

Be ready.

The light begins to fade.

Not quickly, slowly, gently, the way dawn fades the stars. The radiance dims. The figure loses definition, becomes less a shape and more a glow, then less a glow and more a memory of light.

The tide resumes. The waves crash forward, foam hissing across the sand. The stars return to their slow wheel. The world starts again.

Lem stands alone on the beach.

The light is gone. The figure is gone. But the warmth remains, on his face, in his chest, in the place where the knowing was planted.

Tomorrow.

He walks back to his camp. His legs are steadier now. His heart is calm.

He rebuilds the fire. Feeds it driftwood until the flames climb high. Sits beside it, wrapped in his sleeping bag, watching the darkness.

He should stay awake. Should keep watch. Should be ready.

But something has shifted. The preparation is complete. Whatever comes tomorrow will come whether he's awake or asleep. The waiting is over.

The fire burns low. The stars wheel overhead. The waves keep their rhythm.

His eyes grow heavy.

He doesn't fight it.

He lies back on the sand, the sleeping bag pulled around him, the fire crackling softly beside him. The sky fills his vision, all those stars, all that light, the whole universe looking down at him.

He sleeps.

Deep. Dreamless. The first true rest in weeks.

The island holds him. The waves sing to him. The stars keep watch.

And somewhere in the darkness, dawn is coming.

Chapter Nineteen

The Encounter

He wakes before dawn.

The sky is gray in the east, the stars still visible overhead. The waves are steady, rhythmic, the same sound that lulled him to sleep. The fire has gone to ash. The air is cold and smells of salt.

Lem lies still for a moment, wrapped in his sleeping bag, watching the sky lighten. He slept deeply, the first dreamless sleep in weeks. His body feels heavy, rested, strange.

He sits up. The beach stretches empty in both directions. The dunes behind him. The ocean before him. Nothing moves except the water.

He doesn't know what woke him. Only that something did.

He unzips the sleeping bag and stands, stiff from the cold ground. He's still wearing yesterday's clothes, flannel shirt, jeans, the jacket he's had for twenty years. He pulls it tighter and walks toward the water.

The sand is firm near the tideline, packed by the retreating waves. He stops where the foam reaches his boots and stands there, watching the horizon. The light is strengthening. Pink now. Gold at the edges.

He thinks: *I came here for something. I don't know what.*

He thinks: *Maybe nothing will happen. Maybe I'll just go home.*

And then he sees the figure.

Far down the beach, where the light is brightest. A man, walking the tideline. Coming toward him.

Lem's chest tightens. He knows this feeling. He's felt it nine times before this trip.

Another dream, he thinks. *I'll wake soon.*

But the sand is cold under his boots. The wind is real on his face.

He doesn't wake.

The figure keeps coming. Unhurried.

Lem stands frozen. He wants to run. He wants to fall to his knees. He does neither.

A hundred yards. Fifty. Twenty.

And now Lem can see the face.

It's the face from the boat. The child on the shore. The homeless man, the waitress, the woman in the gallery. The face that challenged him in the dark.

All of them. None of them.

Him.

The man stops a few feet away. Simple clothes. Bare feet in the sand. Salt dried white at the hem of his pants. He looks like anyone.

Except for the eyes.

Lem has seen those eyes in every dream. He has reached for them and woken grasping at nothing. He has had nine encounters learning their exact shade, their depth, the way they hold sorrow and joy in equal measure.

Now they are looking at him. And they are not dissolving.

Lem opens his mouth to speak. Nothing comes out.

The man watches him. As if they have all the time in the world.

And Lem begins to weep.

Not sobs. Just tears, streaming down his face. His shoulders don't shake. His breath doesn't catch. The tears simply come, from somewhere deeper than anything he has words for.

The man doesn't move. Doesn't reach for him. Doesn't tell him to stop. He just waits.

Lem weeps for a long time. The sun clears the horizon. The light turns gold. The waves keep their rhythm. The world goes on.

When the tears finally slow, Lem wipes his face with the back of his hand. His voice, when it comes, is hoarse.

"I thought I was losing my mind."

The man tilts his head slightly. Listening.

"I thought... all those nights... I thought something was wrong with me. That I was broken. That I needed to be fixed."

Lem shakes his head slowly.

"But you're real. You were always real."

The man speaks. His voice is quiet, unremarkable, the voice of any man on any beach.

"Yes."

One word. But it lands in Lem's chest like an anchor finding bottom.

"Why?" Lem asks. "Why me? Why any of this?"

The man doesn't answer immediately. He looks out at the water, then back at Lem.

"Walk with me."

He turns and begins to walk along the tideline, the direction he came from. Lem hesitates for a moment, then follows.

They walk in silence. The sand is wet and firm beneath their feet. Small shells crunch. The waves wash in and out, erasing their footprints behind them.

Lem doesn't know how long they walk. Time feels different here, stretched, unhurried. The sun climbs. The air warms. The beach curves gently, and they follow it.

Finally, the man stops. He sits down on the sand, above the tide line, facing the water. After a moment, Lem sits beside him.

They watch the waves together. A pelican glides past, inches above the water, then rises and wheels away.

"You sat in the pews," the man says quietly. "You spoke the words. You received the bread and wine."

Lem nods. His throat is tight.

"That path was real. It formed you. It held you when you needed holding."

"But it wasn't enough," Lem whispers.

"No. You felt something missing. A hollow place you couldn't name."

"I thought it was me. I thought I wasn't believing hard enough. Praying right. I thought..."

He stops. The man waits.

"I thought God had left. That the silence meant He was gone."

The man turns to look at him. Those eyes.

"The silence wasn't absence. It was preparation."

Lem frowns. "I don't understand."

"You couldn't hear me the way you used to. The words had lost their weight." He pauses. "So I came differently."

"In dreams," Lem says.

"In forms you could receive."

"But why?" Lem's voice cracks. "Why the pain? The sleepless nights? The feeling like everything was falling apart?"

The man is quiet for a long moment. When he speaks, his voice is gentle.

"You were tightly closed. The life you'd built had no door I could enter."

"The breaking..." Lem starts.

"Was a door," the man says softly. "The only one you knew how to open."

Lem stares at him. The tears are coming again, but he doesn't try to stop them.

"I didn't choose to break."

"No. You didn't." The man's voice holds something like sorrow. "I'm sorry it hurt so much. It was the only way in, the only door you'd left unlocked."

"I don't break people to hurt them." The man holds Lem's gaze. "I meet them where they break."

The words hang in the air between them. The waves wash in. The sun climbs higher.

"The path they showed you was real," the man says finally. "The path I've shown you is real. They are not enemies. One taught you how to live. The other taught you how to see."

"One formed you. The other is filling you." He pauses. "Both are mine."

Lem looks at the sand. At the water. Everything looks the same, but somehow everything looks different.

"The kingdom is spread out upon the earth," Lem says.

"Yes." The man gestures at the driftwood, the shells, the light on the water. "And now you see it."

Lem looks. And he does see. The ordinary has become radiant, not glowing, not magical, but *present* in a way it wasn't before. As if a veil has been lifted. As if he's been colorblind his whole life and is only now seeing what was always there.

"Split a piece of driftwood," Lem whispers.

"I am there."

"Lift a sea shell."

"You will find me."

They sit in silence.

After a while, the man extends his hands. Palms up. Open.

Lem looks. And he sees.

The scars are there. Not fresh, not bleeding. Healed. But present. The marks of wounds that will never fully disappear.

Lem reaches out slowly. His fingers hover over the man's palm.

"Can I..."

"Yes."

He touches them. The skin is smooth around the edges, slightly raised at the center. Warm. Real.

Real.

The last wall falls.

Lem doesn't know how long he stays like that, his fingers resting on the scars, his head bowed. The man doesn't pull away.

When Lem finally sits back, something has settled in him. Like coming home to a house you didn't know you'd left.

"There were others," the man says. "Who walked with me. Who remembered."

Lem looks up.

"The words they preserved, Matthew, Mark, Luke, John, they are true. But they are not all."

"Thomas," Lem says. "Mary. Philip."

"You were seeking. You found." He turns back to Lem. "Buried is not lost."

"Mary saw first." The man's voice is soft. "They didn't believe her. She told anyway."

"And Thomas," Lem says.

"He doubted. And he was met."

Lem is quiet for a moment. Then:

"There are others like me."

"Many."

The word settles over him.

"They need to know what you have learned," the man says.

Lem shakes his head slowly. "I don't know how..."

"Yes you do."

Lem stares at the water.

"I have to tell them."

The man waits.

"This is what I'm supposed to write."

The man holds his gaze.

Lem nods slowly. "Like Thomas said, if truth isn't brought forth, it turns inward. It destroys you."

"Bring forth what is within you," the man says softly.

"I'm not meant to convince anyone," Lem says. "Am I."

"No. Just to tell what happened. And let it find who it's meant to find."

"Mary told. They didn't believe. She told anyway." The man pauses. "So did Thomas."

"And now I write."

"That is what you know."

The man is quiet for a moment. Then he says:

"There is something else."

Lem waits.

"Last night. On this beach. Before you slept."

Lem's breath catches. The whispers. The weight. The fear and pride and doubt that pressed down on him in the darkness.

"You faced something."

"Yes," Lem says.

"You know what it was."

Lem nods slowly. "Last night it was personal. Like it knew exactly where I was weakest."

"He comes for everyone I call. He came for me, in another wilderness, a long time ago."

Lem looks at him. The man who walked forty days in the desert. Who faced the whisper before any of them.

"I didn't know what to do," Lem says. "I just... prayed. The way I always pray."

"You gave thanks."

The words are simple. But they land in Lem's chest like something falling into place.

"Not victory. Just faithfulness. Not triumph. Just thanks," the man says.

Lem feels tears rising again. He didn't know. He just did what he's always done.

The man reaches out and places his hand on Lem's shoulder. The weight of it is warm. Real.

"That is your greatest strength. The darkness has no answer for a grateful heart."

Lem looks at him. The face he's been chasing through eight dreams. The eyes that have watched him from fishermen and children and waitresses and homeless men. The scars that prove none of this is metaphor.

"I didn't feel like I won anything," Lem says. "I just prayed. And then I slept."

The man nods once.

"It's what I know," Lem says.

"Then do what you know."

He stands. Lem scrambles to his feet.

"Will I see you again?"

The man turns. Looks at him for a long moment.

"Not like this."

Lem's chest tightens.

The man steps closer. "You will not see me like this again. But you will not need to. Now you see me in everything."

He reaches out and pulls Lem into an embrace.

Lem feels arms around him, strong, warm, real. He feels his own arms rise to return the embrace. He buries his face against the man's shoulder and something gives way, the last door, the last distance. Every prayer he ever prayed. Every Sunday morning. Every whispered plea in the dark. All of it answered. All of it held. He is known, and not turned away.

And beneath that, something older. Something he has no memory of but recognizes anyway. He is a child being welcomed home. And it is this. Just this. An embrace on a beach at sunrise.

The man's voice is near his ear.

"Peace be with you."

Then the man steps back.

He holds Lem's eyes for one more moment, and in that moment, Lem sees something vast. Something that has been watching since before the stars and will be watching long after they're gone. Something that knows him utterly and loves him anyway.

Then the man turns.

He walks down the beach. Toward the light.

Lem watches. He doesn't call out. He doesn't try to follow.

He watches until the figure grows small. Until he's a speck against the brightness. Until he can't see it anymore.

The beach is empty.

The waves wash in.

The sun is fully risen now, warm on Lem's face.

He stands there for a long time.

* * *

He walks back down the beach and breaks down his camp slowly, deliberately, as if the motions themselves are sacred.

The walk back across the island is different than the walk out. Yesterday he was seeking. Today he has found.

The wild horses watch him pass, unafraid.

His boat is where he left it. He wades out, climbs aboard, starts the engine.

Shackleford grows smaller. The mainland grows larger.

He's going home. And he knows what he has to do.

Chapter Twenty

Homecoming

Beth doesn't sleep.

She lies in the dark, listening to the house settle around her, the creak of old wood, the hum of the refrigerator, the silence where Lem should be. His side of the bed is empty. Has been empty since yesterday morning, when he loaded his gear into the Pathfinder and left her a note on the kitchen counter.

Down the hall, Kate is sleeping in her old room. Or maybe not sleeping, maybe lying awake like Beth, staring at the ceiling, waiting for morning.

Beth turns onto her side. Stares at Lem's pillow.

She didn't try to stop him. She wanted to, God, she wanted to. Wanted to grab his arm and demand he stay, demand he see the psychiatrist Father John recommended, demand he come back to her, back to the life they'd built, back to *normal*.

But she'd been asleep. He'd slipped out before dawn, quiet as a ghost, leaving nothing but eight words on a piece of paper. *"Gone to Shackleford. I have to do this."*

I have to do this.

Not *I want to.* Not *I've decided to. I have to.* As if something larger than choice was driving him. As if he couldn't have stayed even if he'd wanted to.

She thinks about their conversation last night, her and Kate, sitting at this same kitchen table, holding hands in the dark. Kate had said: "What if Dad is exactly where he's supposed to be, doing exactly what he's supposed to do?"

Beth wants to believe that. Wants to trust that God is still God, even when God works in ways she doesn't understand. But the fear keeps rising, keeps pushing against her faith like water against a dam.

She's never felt so far from Lem. Thirty years of marriage, and she's always known where he was, in his office, on the boat, in the bed beside her. Even when they fought, even when they went days without really talking, she knew the geography of his days. Could picture him at his desk, on the water, in the kitchen making coffee.

But she can't picture him now. Can't see him on that island, in that tent, under those stars. He's in a place she's never been, waiting for something she can't imagine. And all she can do is lie here in the dark and pray.

Please, she whispers. The word rises without thought, the way prayers do in the deepest part of the night. *Please bring him back to me.*

Please let him be okay. Please give me the strength to meet him where he is, not where I want him to be.

She doesn't know if God is listening. She's believed all her life that God listens, believed it in the quiet, steady way she believes most things. But tonight, in the dark, with Lem somewhere beyond her reach, even that certainty feels thin.

She lies awake until the light begins to gray the windows.

* * *

Beth moves through the house like a ghost, making coffee she won't drink, standing at windows, looking at nothing. Duke follows her from room to room, anxious, sensing something wrong. She reaches down absently to scratch behind his ears.

Kate finds her in the kitchen, staring at the water.

"Any word?"

Beth shakes her head. "Nothing."

Kate pours herself a cup of coffee. She's dressed simply, jeans, a sweater, but her face carries the same exhaustion Beth feels. Neither of them slept well.

"He'll come back today," Kate says. "I can feel it."

"How can you feel something like that?"

Kate doesn't answer. Just wraps her hands around her mug and looks out at the water.

The bay is flat and silver in the early light. The dock stretches out toward the empty slip where the Pathfinder should be. The morning is calm, windless, the kind of December day that could go either way, cold and bright, or gray and heavy with rain.

They sit together at the table. Mother and daughter. Waiting.

The knock on the door makes them both jump.

Beth stands. She wasn't expecting anyone. Kate is already here. Bud would call before coming over. The neighbors know better than to drop by unannounced.

She walks to the front door. Opens it.

Father John is standing on the porch.

He's not wearing his collar, just a flannel shirt, khakis, the kind of clothes he wears on his days off. His face is pale. There are shadows under his eyes, the look of a man who hasn't slept well.

"Elizabeth," he says. "May I come in?"

* * *

Beth makes tea because she doesn't know what else to do.

Father John sits at the kitchen table, in the chair across from Kate.

His hands are folded in front of him. He hasn't said why he's here.

Hasn't said much of anything since Beth let him in. Just followed her to the kitchen and sat down, his face carrying something she can't read.

Kate is watching him. Beth can see the concern in her daughter's eyes, not suspicion, but care. Kate has known Father John her whole life. He baptized her, standing beside Lem's father at the font. He watched her serve as an acolyte, heard her sing in the choir, saw her grow from a child into a woman. There's history between them. Affection.

Beth sets a mug in front of him. Sits down beside Kate. Waits.

"I noticed you weren't at church yesterday," he says finally. His eyes move from Beth to Kate and back. "Either of you."

"Lem left for the Banks yesterday morning," Beth says. "I couldn't... I couldn't sit there alone. Not in that pew. Not after everything."

"And I came down to be with Mom," Kate adds. "I drove down last night."

Father John nods slowly. His hands are still folded, but Beth notices they're pressed together tightly. The knuckles white.

"He's still out there? Lem?"

"As far as I know. He took camping gear. Said he had to go." Beth's voice cracks slightly. "He didn't say when he'd be back."

Father John is quiet for a long moment. The clock ticks on the wall. The refrigerator hums. Outside, a gull cries over the water.

"Elizabeth. Kate." He looks at them both, and Beth sees something in his face she's never seen before. Not the priest's composure, the pastoral calm she's relied on for twenty years. Something rawer. More human. "I need to tell you something."

Kate leans forward slightly. Beth feels her daughter's hand find hers under the table.

"I haven't been able to sleep," Father John says. "Since Wednesday. Since Lem sat in my office and told me what's been happening to him."

"I know it was difficult to hear," Beth begins. "I know it sounds,"

"It doesn't sound like anything." His voice is sharper than she's ever heard it. He catches himself, takes a breath, softens. "That's what I need to tell you. It doesn't *sound* like anything, because I've heard it before. Or felt it. The Sunday before, at the communion rail, when I placed the bread in his hands..."

He trails off. His eyes are distant, seeing something that isn't in this kitchen.

"What happened?" Kate asks quietly. Her voice is gentle. The voice she uses with patients, Beth realizes. The voice that invites confession.

"I don't know how to describe it." He shakes his head slowly. "I've been a priest for forty years. I've administered communion thousands of times. It's sacred, yes, I believe that, I've always believed that, but it's also... routine. The motions become automatic. You speak the words, you place the bread, you move on."

He looks at them directly now. His eyes are bright. Wet.

"But when I reached Lem, when I held the wafer over his palm, something happened. My hand began to shake. I couldn't control it. And when I looked at him, when I looked into his eyes..."

His voice breaks. He presses his lips together, fighting for control.

"I saw something, Elizabeth. Kate. Something I can't explain. A light. A presence. Something looking back at me through your husband's eyes, through your father's eyes, that was not, that was *more* than, just Lem."

Beth's heart is pounding. She doesn't speak. Doesn't move. Beside her, Kate is very still.

"I felt it," Father John continues. "In my chest. In my bones. The same thing I felt when I was ordained, when the bishop laid hands on me and I *knew, knew,* that I was being called. That certainty. That absolute, unshakeable certainty."

He's weeping now. The tears streaming down his face, unwiped. Beth has never seen Father John cry. In thirty years, through funerals and hospital visits and moments of profound grief, she's never seen him break like this.

"And then Lem came to my office. And he told me about the dreams. The visitors. The words they spoke. And I knew, God help me, I *knew,* that he was telling the truth. That something real was happening to him. Something holy."

His hands have unclenched. They're resting on the table now, open, empty.

"And I told him to see a psychiatrist."

The words fall into the silence like stones into still water.

"I told him he might be having a breakdown. That we shouldn't rule out medical causes. That the church is *cautious* about these things." He laughs, a short, bitter sound. "Cautious. Forty years a priest, and when Christ finally, *finally*, shows up in my parish, I tell the man to go see a doctor."

Beth is crying too now. She didn't know when she started. The tears are just there, streaming down her face, falling onto the table.

Kate stands. Moves around the table. And Beth watches as her daughter, her brilliant, skeptical, scientifically trained daughter, puts her arms around Father John and holds him.

"You were scared," Kate says softly. "We've all been scared. Mom and me, we've been looking for explanations too. Something we could understand. Something we could fix."

Father John's shoulders shake. He's weeping openly now, his face buried in his hands, Kate's arms around him.

"I've known you my whole life," Kate continues. "You helped baptize me. You watched me grow up. You're a good man, Father. A good priest. And you made a mistake. That's all. You made a mistake because you were human, and this is terrifying, and none of us knows what to do with it."

Beth watches her daughter comfort the priest who comforted her through childhood, through scraped knees and teenage heartbreak and the death of her grandfather. The circle completing itself. The student becoming the teacher.

Father John raises his head. Wipes his face with the back of his hand.

Looks at Kate with something like wonder.

"When did you get so wise?"

"I'm not wise. I'm just as lost as you are." Kate returns to her seat, but she keeps her hand on his arm. "I just know that Dad needs us to believe him. Not to understand, I don't think any of us can understand.

But to believe him. To be with him."

Beth finds her voice. "Why, Father?" she whispers. "If you knew, if you felt it, why didn't you say something?"

Father John looks at her. His face is ravaged, stripped of all pretense.

"Because I was afraid."

He says it simply. Without excuse.

"Because admitting that Lem was telling the truth would mean admitting that everything I thought I understood about God, about how He works, how He appears, what He asks, was incomplete. Would mean admitting that my careful liturgies, my approved channels for the divine... were just one small piece of something much larger."

He shakes his head slowly.

"I've spent my whole life building a house for God to live in. And then God showed up somewhere else, on a fishing boat, in a child's scarred hands, in the eyes of a parishioner I've known for thirty years, and I didn't know what to do with that. It terrified me. So I did what afraid people do. I looked for an explanation that would make it go away."

He pauses. When he speaks again, his voice is different. Quieter. The voice of a priest who has finally found solid ground.

"But I know what this is now. What's been happening to all of us. I've seen it before, not this dramatic, not this clear, but I've seen the pattern. In forty years of ministry, sitting with people in crisis, I've learned to recognize it."

Beth looks at him. "Recognize what?"

"The enemy's work."

The word lands in the kitchen like a stone.

Kate's hand tightens on Father John's arm. Beth feels her breath catch.

"I don't mean possession. Nothing dramatic. He's subtler than that. He works through ordinary things. Reasonable things."

He looks at Beth directly.

"Fear. That's his first weapon. The fear that Lem is broken. The fear that we're losing him."

Beth feels the words land. The fear she's been carrying for weeks suddenly has a name.

"He used fear on me at the communion rail. I felt the truth, and immediately the fear came. It pushed me away from what I knew."

"And pride. That's his second weapon. I told Lem to see a psychiatrist partly because I was afraid, but partly because I didn't want to be the priest with the crazy parishioner."

Kate nods slowly. Beth can see recognition in her daughter's face, the physician who worried about what her colleagues would think if her father claimed to see Christ.

"And doubt." Father John's voice is gentle now. "The third weapon. The whisper that says: What if none of this is real? What if you're all being foolish? The doubt that makes us question our own experience."

"That makes us reach for explanations that feel safer than the truth."

He looks at both of them.

"Fear. Pride. Doubt. He's been using them on us since the moment Lem started dreaming."

Beth wipes her face. Her whole body is trembling.

"I've been feeling all of that," she says. "But I didn't know... I just thought I was struggling."

"It's not your fault." Father John reaches across the table and takes her hands. "He takes our love and turns it into fear. Takes our care for each other and makes us want to fix instead of follow."

"Then how do we fight it?" Kate asks. "If we didn't even know it was happening, how do we stop it?"

Father John is quiet for a moment.

"There's only one thing that defeats him. I've seen it in forty years of ministry."

He looks at them both.

"Gratitude."

The word hangs in the air. Simple. Almost too simple.

"The enemy cannot exist in the same space as a grateful heart." Father John squeezes Beth's hands. "I don't know the theology of it. But I've watched it happen. Gratitude isn't just a feeling. It's a weapon."

Beth closes her eyes. She thinks about all the mornings she's watched Lem thank God over a fish, over a meal, over the simple gift of another day.

Maybe that's why Christ came to him. Maybe gratitude was the door that was never locked.

"I've been praying for him to come back to normal," she says. "But maybe that's not what I should be praying for."

"Maybe he's supposed to go forward," Kate says. "And we're supposed to go with him."

"There is no diagnosis." Father John's voice is gentle now. Broken, but gentle. "Your husband is not sick. He's not having a breakdown. He's being visited. Called. Chosen for something."

He looks at both of them.

"And we can either let fear and pride and doubt keep us from joining him, or we can answer those weapons with the only thing that defeats them."

"Gratitude," Beth whispers.

"Gratitude."

He releases her hands. Looks at them with something that wasn't there when he walked in, not certainty, but peace.

"Can we pray together? Not the formal prayers. Just... thanking God."

Beth looks at Kate. Kate nods.

They bow their heads.

And Father John begins, not with the familiar liturgical phrases, but simply: "Thank you. Thank you for Lem. For the gratitude that has always marked his life. Thank you that you chose him, whatever that means, whatever it costs. Thank you that he said yes."

"Thank you for Beth. For thirty years of love strong enough to follow even when it can't understand."

"Thank you for Kate. For her mind and her heart. Thank you that she believed her father on the boat.

"Thank you for the fear, because it shows us how much we love him. Thank you for the pride we're laying down."

"Thank you that you are God. That you work in ways we don't understand."

"Thank you."

He falls silent.

The kitchen is still. The clock ticks. The sun climbs higher outside the window.

Beth feels something shift in her chest. Not the fear disappearing, it's still there, underneath, but something stronger rising to meet it. Something that feels like peace. Like trust. Like the first breath after being underwater too long.

She opens her eyes. Looks at Father John. Looks at Kate.

They're all crying. All three of them. But it's different now. The tears aren't grief, aren't fear, aren't confusion.

They're relief.

"Thank you," Beth whispers. "For coming. For sharing this with us."

Father John nods. His face is calmer now. The ravaged look is gone, replaced by something quieter. As if the breaking has made room for something new.

"When he comes back, we meet him with faith, not fear. We don't try to fix him or explain him."

"We just be with him," Kate says.

"Yes."

* * *

They sit together for a long time. The tea grows cold. None of them moves to leave.

The waiting feels different now. Full of thanks.

Kate sits quietly. There's a peace about her that Beth didn't expect. She believed her father on the boat. She wavered. And now she's found her footing again.

Father John stares out at the water. He looks older. Or maybe just more honest.

"I need to ask his forgiveness," he says.

"He'll give it," Beth says. "That's who he is."

Father John nods slowly.

The sun is higher now, the water brightening from silver to blue.

Beth stands. Pours out the cold tea. Makes a fresh pot.

She's pouring when Father John speaks.

"Elizabeth."

He's standing at the window, his hand pressed against the glass.

"Look."

Beth moves to the window.

Out on the sound, far out, where the water meets the sky, a boat. Small at this distance. But she knows its shape. Knows the angle of the console, the line of the hull.

The Pathfinder.

Coming home.

* * *

They walk down the dock together.

Beth's heart is hammering. Kate is beside her, shoulder to shoulder. Behind them, Father John.

Everyone who struggled. Everyone who doubted. Everyone who loved him anyway.

The boat grows larger. Beth can see Lem now, standing at the console, one hand on the wheel. He looks the same. He looks completely different.

Peace. He looks like a man who has found peace.

He cuts the engine. The Pathfinder glides the last few yards, easing up to the dock with the practiced grace of a thousand arrivals.

Lem looks up. His eyes find Beth first.

She feels the tears start again.

Then his gaze moves to Kate. His face softens. Something unspoken passes between father and daughter, the bond that's always been there, deeper than language, stronger than doubt.

Then Father John.

And Lem doesn't look surprised.

He picks up the bowline. Steps onto the dock. Ties off the boat, his hands moving through the familiar motions.

Father John steps forward.

"Lem."

Lem straightens.

The two men stand there, the priest and the fisherman, the one who turned away and the one who was turned from.

"I was wrong." Father John's voice is steady, but his eyes are bright with tears. "At the communion rail, I felt something. I knew. And I turned away from it."

Lem listens.

"All I can do is ask you to forgive me."

For a long moment, Lem doesn't speak.

Then he steps forward and embraces the priest.

"There's nothing to forgive," Lem says. "You were human. That's all."

Father John's shoulders shake. He's weeping, but differently now. With release.

Lem holds him until the shaking stops. Then he steps back.

"Go home. Rest. We'll talk soon."

Father John nods. Wipes his face. Then he turns and walks up the dock, past Beth and Kate. The steps of a man who has laid down a burden.

* * *

Kate moves next.

She doesn't say anything. Just walks toward her father and wraps her arms around him, the way she did on the boat that afternoon when she said *I believe you*, the way she did when she was a little girl and he was the center of her world.

She holds him for a long time. And Lem holds her back.

Beth watches them, father and daughter, the two people she loves most in the world. She can see Kate's shoulders trembling, can see Lem's hand come up to cradle the back of his daughter's head, the gesture he's made since she was an infant.

They don't speak. They don't need to.

Everything Kate has felt these past weeks, the belief and the doubt, the fear and the hope, the love that outlasted all of it, is there in the embrace. And everything Lem knows about his daughter, her strength, her skepticism, her fierce heart, is there in how he holds her.

When Kate finally pulls back, her face is wet but she's smiling.

"Welcome home, Dad."

"Good to be home, Katie."

She steps aside. And it's Beth's turn.

* * *

She looks at her husband.

This man she's loved for thirty years. This man who left her a note on the kitchen counter and walked into the unknown.

He looks back at her. And she sees it, everything that's changed and everything that hasn't. He's not the same man who left.

But he's still *her* man. Still Lem.

The fear is still there, faint now, like an echo. She doesn't understand what's happened to him. Doesn't know what it will cost.

But the gratitude is stronger.

Thank you that he's here. Thank you that I get to love him, whatever comes next.

She steps forward. Into his arms. Into whatever comes next.

He holds her. His arms around her, his cheek against her hair, his heart beating steady against hers. She smells salt and smoke and something else, something clean, like the air after a storm.

She says what matters.

"I'm with you."

"I know," Lem says.

She pulls back. Touches his face, making sure he's real.

"Tell me," she says. "Everything."

"I will."

He takes her hand. They turn toward the house. Kate falls into step beside them, the family that almost broke and didn't.

Behind them, the Pathfinder rocks gently in its slip. The water catches the light and sends it scattering across the hull. The world goes on, the pelicans diving, the gulls crying, the tide doing what the tide has done for millennia.

But something has changed.

Something has begun.

Chapter Twenty-One

The Testimony

They reach the house together, Beth on one side, Kate on the other, their arms linked through his.

Duke is waiting at the door, tail wagging, pressing against Lem's legs as soon as they step inside. Lem kneels down, scratches behind the dog's ears, lets Duke lick his face.

"Hey, boy. I'm home."

He stands. Beth is watching him. Kate is watching him. Both of them waiting.

"There's something I have to do," he says quietly.

Beth's hand finds his. "Now?"

"Now." He squeezes her fingers. "I know what I'm supposed to write."

She searches his face. Whatever she sees there, it's enough. She nods.

"Go," she says. "We'll be here."

He turns. Walks down the hall. Past the kitchen, past the living room, past all the familiar spaces of the life he's lived for thirty years.

He stops at the door of his office.

* * *

The room is small. Barely big enough for the desk, the chair, the bookshelf stuffed with paperbacks and research volumes. But it has the window, the window that looks out over the bay, over the dock, over the boat.

He steps inside. Closes the door behind him.

The laptop is where he left it. Closed. Waiting.

He sits down. Opens it. The screen glows to life.

The document is there, the same empty outline, the same scattered notes, the same white space he's been staring at for months. The book that wouldn't come.

He selects all. Deletes.

A blank page.

The cursor blinks.

And Lem doesn't move.

* * *

He sits there, hands resting on the keyboard, staring at the white screen.

But he's not seeing it.

He's seeing the beach.

The figure walking toward him in the dawn light. The face that had flickered through nine encounters, always dissolving before it could be known. But not this morning. This morning, the face held. The eyes met his and didn't look away.

He walked with Christ.

The words form in his mind, and they stagger him. He walked with Christ. On a beach in North Carolina, in the twenty-first century, a fisherman from Beaufort walked beside the risen Lord and listened to him speak.

No one will believe it. He barely believes it himself, sitting here in this ordinary room, in this ordinary life. But it happened. The sand was real beneath his feet. The voice was real in his ears. The scars were real beneath his fingers.

He takes a breath. Deep. Slow. Feels it fill his chest, then release.

Another breath.

The tears come.

Not grief. Not relief. Something he has no name for, the overflow of a vessel filled beyond capacity. The tears stream down his face and he lets them fall, doesn't wipe them away, doesn't try to stop them.

He thinks about the gifts.

Nine encounters. Teachings offered to him like bread broken and shared.

The kingdom is spread out upon the earth, and people do not see it. But now he sees it.

Why do you hold so tightly to what washes away? The child on the shore, scarred hands shaping sand he would never keep. Everything Lem has been gripping, his old life, his old self, the man Beth married, it all washes away. Let it.

Truth comes in types and images because the naked truth would destroy. The disguises are mercy.

Bring forth what is within you, and it will save you. Keep it hidden, and it will destroy you. He cannot keep this hidden.

Mary saw first, and they didn't believe her. She told anyway. He must tell anyway.

The voices that were buried for sixteen centuries rose again. Buried is not lost.

If the Savior made her worthy, who are you to reject her? The chain is unbroken. Bud defending Lem. Levi defending Mary. The same words across two thousand years.

Love bears all things. Beth. Kate. Father John. Bearing what they couldn't understand because they loved him.

And gratitude: gratitude is the weapon the enemy cannot answer. The whisper stopped. The darkness lifted. Because he gave thanks.

Pieces of a teaching so old and so new that the church buried half of it and forgot the rest. Given to him. Entrusted to him. A fisherman. A writer. A man who never asked for any of it.

He bows his head.

The prayer rises without effort, the way it has risen over a thousand fish, a thousand meals, a thousand ordinary moments that were never ordinary at all.

Thank you.

Thank you for coming to me. Thank you for not giving up when I doubted, when I was afraid, when I thought I was losing my mind. Thank you for the dreams that broke me open. Thank you for the teachings that filled me.

Thank you for walking with me on that beach. Thank you for your voice. Thank you for your patience. Thank you for sitting beside me in the sand and explaining what I couldn't understand.

Thank you for letting me see your face.

Thank you for the scars. For holding out your hands. For letting me touch them. For proving it was real when I needed proof. That you were real. That you are real.

Thank you for the commission. For trusting me with something so unfathomably large. For believing I could carry what I cannot carry.

Thank you for Beth. For Kate. For Bud. For Father John. Thank you for the people who loved me through this. Thank you for the ones who will read what I write and recognize the truth in it.

Thank you.

He breathes.

The tears slow. Something settles in his chest, not peace exactly, but clarity. The noise in his mind has gone quiet. The static has faded. There is only this: the white page, the blinking cursor, and the story waiting to be told.

He is so small. A man in a little room looking out at the water. Nobody special. Nobody important. The same hands that have hauled nets and gutted fish and held his wife in the dark.

And yet those hands touched the scars of Christ.

He doesn't understand why. Doesn't know why him, why now, why any of it. But understanding isn't his burden to carry.

His burden is to tell.

Mary told. They didn't believe her. She told anyway.

Thomas went. He traveled to the ends of the earth, carrying the teaching. Many turned away. He told anyway.

And now Lem.

He places his fingers on the keys.

The words come the way the water comes, from somewhere he cannot see, toward a shore he has always known.

He begins. He writes.

* * *

He becomes aware of the water before he becomes aware of himself.

The boat is moving. He feels it before he understands it: the slow, steady glide beneath his feet, the faint hum of the trolling motor carrying them forward. He is standing on the bow of his Pathfinder, barefoot on the casting deck, the rod already in his hands. Cool and damp. He doesn't remember stepping onto it.

The marsh slides past on his right. Marsh grass, thick and tall, glowing a pale lime green in the early light. He knows this place: the shallow bay where the water thins over sandy mud, grass and shell, where redfish tail in the shallows and herons stand like gray sentinels at the water's edge. He has worked this shoreline more times than he can count. Since his college days. Since before he understood that some places become part of you.

But something is different this morning.

The sky.

He looks up, and his breath catches.

The sun has not yet broken the horizon, but the light is already filling the sky in ways he has never seen. Colors that don't belong to dawn: deep golds bleeding into violet, ribbons of pale rose and amber stretching across the water. The light seems to come from everywhere and nowhere, pooling in the mist that hangs low over the marsh, turning the marsh grass luminous.

It is the most beautiful morning he has ever seen.

And he knows, somewhere beneath thought, that this is not real. That mornings do not look like this. That he is dreaming...

About the author

Bobby Bryan Goodwin is a 100-ton Master Captain, waterman, and coastal storyteller. Educated at the University of North Carolina at Chapel Hill, he has spent decades creating and producing regional and maritime television, including *Down East Outdoors* and *Big Rock TV*. His creative work spans novels, screenplays, television, and film, often rooted in coastal history, outdoor life, and the enduring pull of Southern maritime heritage.

An eighth-generation native of North Carolina's Southern Outer Banks and a lifelong fisherman, he makes his home in Beaufort, where stories of tide, memory, and faith continue to shape his work. *The Apostle* is his second novel. His debut, *King Tide: A Southern Outer Banks Novel*, is also available.